MURDER AT NINE FINGERS CHARLIE'S ART EMPORIUM

A Saugatuck Murder Mystery

by

G Corwin Stoppel

Lord Hiltensweiller Press

The Saugatuck Murder Mystery Series

The Great Saugatuck Murder Mystery

Death by Palette Knife

A Murder of Crows

The Murder of the Saugatuck Yarn Hoarder

Murder on the Saugatuck Chain Ferry

Murder at Nine Fingers Charlie's Art Emporium

First Edition

Published by Lord Hiltensweiller Press, Saugatuck, Michigan, 49453
lordhilt@gmail.com

Cover design by S. Winthers

ISBN: 9798627859781

Imprint: Independently published

In memory of three great friends who
gave so much of themselves to Saugatuck —
David Balas, Henry Gleason, and Bill Galligan.

Disclaimer

This is a work of fiction.
The characters are fictional, except for Henry and Bobbie, and they were far too young to have been around when none of this ever happened. Any similarity to any real person is merely a figment of your imagination.

Acknowledgements

Once again I am deeply indebted to John Thomas and Peter Schakel for proof-reading and editing, as well as their suggestions; to Sally Winthers who magically makes a manuscript turn into a book; and to my wonderful wife Pat Dewey for all her support and advice.

This time round, I came home with the exciting news that there was a vacant store for rent, and a friend and I had the great idea of opening an art gallery I would call "Nine Fingers Charlie's Art Emporium." She wanted to know why I would call it that. I explained we didn't know anything about art or running a gallery, but with a name like that people would be curious and come in. She looked at me and said, "The fastest way to lose money is to open an art gallery; make it into a book." Probably some very good advice!

INTRODUCTION

FROM AN OLD UNDATED LETTER FOUND IN PHOEBE'S STEAMER TRUNK:

The mournful wail of a foghorn still sends shivers up and down my back. That is because I grew up in Saugatuck, Michigan, and there was a huge horn at the breakwater where the mouth of the Kalamazoo River enters Lake Michigan. It was several miles from town, but we could hear it clearly, and we knew that a fogbank was marching toward us, and danger was looming. Boaters, whether they were Sunday afternoon sailors or the captains of merchant and passenger ships, understood the horn's message.

For those of us in town, even if our feet were planted firmly on the ground, we would feel a cold chill run up and down our spines. We would silently try to remember any friend or family member who was out on the water. I could never remember the formal, stately petitions from the Book of Common Prayer about protecting those in danger on the sea, but in such moments, I got straight to the point, "God, watch out for...."

I still think of my grandfather's words. "The lake is a big body of water with a grave carved in it." And that from a man who was never happier than when he was on the water.

There is another kind of fog that creeps in around us. As a young girl, it was the day of a big test at school, or the Friday afternoon spelling bee. It was when I watched Grandfather Horace waving from the stern of his Aurora, while I wondered if I would see him again the next summer. It was a lot of things, and sometimes, as I got older, I felt I was merely lurching from one gloomy fog bank to the next.

Fog came over us on August 6th. That was the year that Grandfather had solved the mysterious death of Fairy Nightshade, Saugatuck's most despised acid-tongued gossip and yarn hoarder. Then he had turned right around and solved the murder of a young man found dead in the storage box of the Saugatuck Chain Ferry. And I know it was the sixth of August because I had been invited to my best friend's birthday party. Patty and I were the same age, but my birthday was a week later, so she had a fine time reminding me that she was now older. A few decades later I rubbed it in, reminding her that she was ever so much older than I.!

That morning I woke up to the sound of an airplane flying overhead. I didn't think anything more about it, but when I walked up the gangplank to my grandfather's boat, the fog crashed in.

"Before you ask, Doctor Howell returned home," Grandfather said, his lips tight. "Home to Minnesota," he added.

"But she didn't even say goodbye!" I wailed, fighting back a rising lump in my throat. "Is she coming back?"

"Now, there's the real question. I have no idea. She's her own woman." With that, he pulled up his newspaper and hid behind the business section. I felt like he was shutting me out, just as she had shut him out.

The fog wrapped around us like church mold, and it stayed that way until school started the following month. It was a cold, clammy feeling, and I didn't like it.

During that time we were like boats in the Kalamazoo River during a heavy fog. We wanted to make progress, but we kept bumping into each other. We kept getting mixed up with important messages, or missing them all together. Bobbie, the telephone switchboard operator said it best of all, "You got your wires crossed."

I sure did – get my wires crossed, that is. We all had a part in the confusion and muddle and I did my part right from the start.

ONE

For a week Horace had been unusually quiet and distant. Beatrix's sudden departure had something to do with it, of course. He was at loose ends without her teasing and sharp wit, their walks to the soda fountain for ice crème, and long conversations. There was more to it than just her absence. What laid him low was the news about the two gunmen that Bugs Moran had sent to Saugatuck to kill Charlie Haggerty. Chief Garrison had arrested the gunmen and was holding them for trial. While Horace and Beatrix were in Chicago asking for help from Colonel McCormick and the *Chicago Tribune,* a crooked lawyer arrived, waving an extradition order signed by a well-bribed Chicago judge. They were hustled out of town, across the border into Indiana, and were back in Chicago by dinner. Before Horace, Beatrix, and the colonel could get organized, the charges had been dropped.

"Haggerty might have been a crook and a conman, but he deserved justice," Horace said quietly when he heard the news. Theo agreed, and in time Beatrix added, "There is too much pain."

"Too much pain" explained her sudden departure.

"It sure has taken the wind out of his sails," Fred whispered to Harriet and Phoebe. "He's be-calmed, and no mistake about it."

"What can we do?" Phoebe asked. "I hate seeing Grandfather like this."

"Best thing is to just let him be for a while. I've seen it before; so has Doc Theo and his missus. He'll pull out of it, same as always, but on his own time."

"Are you sure?" Harriet asked.

"Oh sure," Fred answered. "Why I've seen him take a hard rap or two, shake it off, and get right back to work. Don't you worry about the boss."

His answer froze Phoebe. Grandfather wasn't working any more. He was a retired surgeon now. There wasn't any work for him to do that would take his mind off of things. His motto had always been that there was no fun like work. And she remembered how he had taught her to make herself useful to others. Now, as she looked at him across the deck, leaning against the rail on the river side, smoking his pipe, he seemed old, tired, diminished. He barely moved and she knew his mind was somewhere else.

Then she shivered. She remembered a story he had told her about his grandmother. "Hot August afternoons, she'd sit out on the front porch doing handwork. Might be darning a sock or shelling peas, or something else. She always made herself useful even if she was sitting down. Now, if she was sitting so she faced the avenue, it meant anyone passing by was welcome to come up and sit for a while and talk. If she was sitting sideways to the avenue, then it meant you could say hello, but keep on walking. And if she was sitting with her back to the street, then it meant, 'don't even think about it, buster.' That applied to family, friends, and strangers."

What made the girl shiver was that his back was to the rest of the family and all of Saugatuck.

Sometimes it seemed as if her aunt Clarice could read minds. She had slowly walked over to where the two women and Fred were talking. "Phoebe, I know you're worried about your grandfather, but just give him time. He still loves you, you know, and some things just can't be fixed. Give him time. You're the one in the waiting room right now, and it's no fun, is it?" She asked.

Phoebe impatiently waited two and a half days until, on the third morning, she exploded, "Thunderation! I'm through sitting in the waiting room."

She had walked about half a block from her home toward the *Aurora* when Peter Landis, the local physician's oldest son, came flying out of a driveway on his bicycle and nearly knocked her over. "Sorry, Phoebe!" he shouted over his left shoulder as he raced down the street.

"Just wait until I see your fa...," she started to shout at him, her right fist raised in anger. She froze, mouth open, arm raised, right in the middle of the sidewalk. It was the biggest, best, most wonderful brainwave of all time. She needed to see him right away! Phoebe picked up her pace and walked quickly toward the *Aurora*. To her relief Horace's LaSalle automobile was parked near the gangway. Even better, Fred was there, polishing the hood ornament.

"Fred, I need your help, please," Phoebe panted. "Can you drive me to Doctor Landis' office?"

He looked alarm. "Everything all right, Phoebe?" he asked. "You feeling okay? Anything ailing you?"

"Yes. It's not that. I'm perfectly fine. No, this is something else and it's really important."

"I got me an idea that this might have something to do with Doc Horace. If you got an idea how to make him feel like his old self again, I'm all for it. We'll catch Doc Landis at the hospital this time of the morning. Probably in the kitchen having a cup of coffee. Hop in!" He touched the brim of his hat as she slid into the back seat.

Fred watched as she marched to the back door of the cottage hospital and headed straight for the kitchen. "Well, this is a surprise, Phoebe? Everything okay? You all right?"

"I am perfectly well, thank you," she said graciously. "I've come about my grandfather. I have kept him under close observation ever since he returned from Chicago, and he is not his usual self."

"You don't mean he's taken to telling jokes or playing the bassoon?" he teased.

Phoebe glared at him, her eyes narrowing. "I am quite serious. I have observed that he is despondent and listless, and those are indications of depression. I haven't consulted with anyone, but I am diagnosing serious depression."

Doctor Landis waved her to a nearby chair. "And do you have a prescription?"

"Yes, as a matter of fact I do. And it is one that you will agree is mutually beneficial. I have heard you talking about how you would like to spend more time with your sons. I am also sure they would benefit from spending more time with you. Well, if you would hire Grandfather to assist you part time, you would have more time for your family, and Grandfather would have something to do to take him out of himself."

Doctor Landis rubbed his chin. "Clear observation. Good work, Phoebe, and a practical diagnosis for treatment. Well done. Very well done. And, I think you are right on the mark. I am more than willing to be your first assistant with your patient. Tell you what, this evening I'll stop round to see him and by hook or crook, we'll get him back in a white jacket with a stethoscope around his neck. Count on it."

"Thank you, Doctor Landis," she said quietly.

"No, thank you. I think very highly of your grandfather. He's a truly great man. So is your uncle Theo. And you're doing me a favor if I can get him to come to our little hospital."

Phoebe leaned closer and whispered, "There's something more, but it doesn't make sense. Just before Mr. Haggerty was killed, I overheard the grown-ups talking about how some young turkeys back home were hoping to kill off Grandfather and Uncle Theo."

The doctor's eyes widened. "Well, I think you heard them say 'young Turks', not turkeys. It's an expression when younger men try to force the older ones to retire. So, I wouldn't be too worried about that. But, at the same time, it is probably something else that has depressed him. I'll keep an eye open for it." He gave her a big smile. "Don't you worry."

Phoebe laughed to herself as she went out the back door. Her grandfather and uncle "great men"? Maybe others thought of them that way, but to her they were her family, and that was what really mattered. From the car, Fred could see that she had been successful. It didn't surprise him when she told him she wanted to be dropped off at Parrish Drugstore. He thought she was probably going to celebrate with a root beer. She walked in through the back door, down the aisles toward the front, and out the door.

Her destination was the Western Union office. Mr. Higgins, the agent, looked up when he heard the bell over the door. "How can I help you?" he asked.

"I saw your advertisement in the Commercial Record. You're looking for a relief telegrapher, and I am here to apply for the job."

He slowly pulled the green visor from his forehead, pulled off his glasses and wiped them with a handkerchief. It was his way to stall for time while he was thinking. "Well, A and One, you're a girl, and I haven't heard of a girl telegrapher since the war. And then B and Two, you have to be able to send and receive Morse Code. You ever heard of the Morse Code?"

"Yes, Mr. Higgins. I can send at twenty-eight and copy at thirty. If I had one of the new butterfly keys I'm sure I could be even faster, but then I might be too fast for some of the other agents," Phoebe said with a smile.

"Twenty eight and thirty, you say? Well, C and Three, you're awfully young to be working, aren't you?"

"I don't think so. Besides I'll show you what I can do and if you hire me then you'll get the bragging rights for having hired the fastest and youngest woman telegrapher in the Upper Midwest, maybe the nation."

"All right, I'll give you a shot." Mr. Higgins sat down at the key and typed out, "Code speed test. Anyone available for test traffic?"

The machine began to clatter. "All right, Miss Walters, your turn. You're talking with Jess Madsen down to New Buffalo. See if you can stump him."

Phoebe sat down at the desk and went to work. "Good morning, Mr. Madsen. This is Phoebe Walters at the Saugatuck station doing a speed test. Did you copy?"

"Course I did. I know you. You have a ham license and I do crossword puzzles in Latin," he sent back. "Have Higgins dictate and send it out cold."

Phoebe nodded to Mr. Higgins who began talking. He was slow, conversational, at first, then began to speed up, trying to make Phoebe crash. Finally, he ran out of breath and quit. "Well, ask Jess how you did?"

"What the devil was that gibberish you sent me?" he replied.

"You said that you were studying Latin, so I translated what Mr. Higgins said into Latin for you, and then sent it," she clicked back.

Mr. Higgins had listened in on the two telegraphers. At first he didn't know what to say. Finally, he muttered, "Well, looks like I got myself bragging rights for hiring the youngest, fastest Latin spewing female telegrapher in the entire these here United States. You got yourself a job young-lady. Afternoons until school starts and then Saturday mornings. I'm starting you out at thirty five cents an hour. And I don't want to hear no complaining about you sending a message in Latin or any other other language other than good old fashioned American English. You read me?"

"Loud and clear. Copy. You're coming in S-9 as we say on the radio."

"Tomorrow, twelve o'clock noon," he reminded her.

Phoebe walked back to the *Aurora* with a big smile on her face. It wasn't even eleven o'clock in the morning and she already had two solid triumphs to her credit. There was no telling what the afternoon would bring. She wouldn't be able say anything about her conversation with Dr. Landis, but then, neither could she wait to tell her grandfather about her job at Western Union.

TWO

At just about the same moment that Phoebe walked into the Western Union station, Doctor Horace stormed into the galley of his boat. "Mrs. Garwood, there is an entire boat for your hired girl to clean, so why is she dead set about cleaning my study right now?" Horace asked sharply.

"And you have an entire boat at your disposal, so you can stay out of your study for however long it takes her to get the job done!" his cook and housekeeper replied. "Why don't you think about stretching your legs for a change? You've been lolly-gagging and moping around here for days. Go see the sights of Saugatuck. You already got your summer suit on, so you're officially presentable in town. In fact, I dare you to have an adventure that puts a smile on your face! And don't forget your hat!"

He glared at her. "This is mutiny, you know. Thunderation! That's what they did to Captain Bligh, you know!" She was not intimidated by his attitude, and smiled when he began to back down. Doctor Horace slapped his left hand against his jacket pocket to make sure he had his pipe and tobacco pouch, did a sharp military about-face, and marched out. "Thunderation, that woman!" he said to himself as he walked down the gangplank to the street. "Thunderation!" he barked aloud, hoping she would hear it.

He walked quickly down the sidewalk, trying to burn off his anger and frustration from the last week. At the end of Water Street, he turned toward Butler, and began his way toward the big hotel. It was only when he got to the Post Office that he cooled down and noticed a new business had opened. "Who in thunderation would call his place 'Nine Finger Charlie's Art Emporium?'" he growled to himself. Without noticing the help wanted sign on the door window, he walked inside to look around.

"Good morning!" a thin, raspy voice came from the back room of the shop. "Be right with you." Horace waited and looked around the little shop. One wall displayed a few small paintings; the other two were still bare. There was a small wooden desk littered with wire, small nails, and a hammer, and a couple of chairs, and not much else. At least the paintings were interesting, if only because Horace recognized the location. Many of them appeared to be of the lagoon at the Ox-Bow art school. Others were waterscapes and dunes. With only a scant knowledge of artists, Horace didn't recognize any of the signatures.

"Find something appealing to you?" the owner asked as he came into the main room. "I'm Charlie Larsen, the proprietor." He had warm smile. He was a tall, thin older man with a van Dyke beard. If he had been on the street or anywhere else, Horace might have taken him for a retired college professor in a light weight three piece summer suit.

"Interesting name for an art gallery," Horace said quietly.

"Well, the truth of the matter is I don't know all that much about art, except that some paintings I like and some I don't. And I know even less about running a gallery. So, I came up with the name based on this." He held up his hands to reveal a missing little finger on his left hand. "Nine Fingers Charlie is what they called me back home, so I figured it would be a catchy handle for a gallery. People will see it and wonder what sort of place it is. They come in, I turn on my irresistible charm, and with a bit of luck, I sell a painting or two."

Horace gave a wintery smile. "I admire your creativity."

"Now tell me, are you here to buy a painting or ask for a job?" Nine Fingers asked.

"Ask about a job?"

"Guess you missed the sign on the door. I'm hiring an assistant. It's part time and I'm paying seventy-five cents an hour plus a commission on every painting you sell. You look like a fellow who knows how to deal with the public. You might add a bit of class to the place," Charlie told him. "And, I'll bet you know your way around a broom and shop brush, too."

Horace rubbed his right hand over his chin. "Seventy-five cents an hour, you say? Plus commission?"

"I figure that's fair. Now, if things are a bit quiet you might like to sweep out the place, dust the paintings and things like that. Nothing too strenuous. I provide a shop apron, too."

Something snapped and crackled in Horace's mind, and for some very peculiar reason the idea of working in an art gallery suddenly appealed to him. He was bored, and he knew it. He didn't need to earn a living, but this would give him something to do. He smiled, thinking about Theo and Clarice's reaction when they heard about it. Harriet too! They would have a fit. The only one who would cheer him on would be Phoebe. Besides, if it didn't work out he could always quit. Moreover, if he was fired, well, he'd been unceremoniously shoved out the door of his own medical practice; being kicked to the curb by a nine-fingered art shop owner couldn't be any worse.

Horace stuck out his right hand. "You've got yourself a salesman, duster, and floor sweeper. I'll accept your offer. Now, when do we get to work?"

"Well, if I were you, and I'm not, but if I were, I would take off that nice suit jacket and put on that shop apron, and then give me a hand putting up some more pictures," Nine Fingers said. "What I'm thinking is that I could use a good man in the mornings. That'll give you the afternoon off to nap or do what you want to do. Might as well get started now."

"Right away, Boss," Horace smiled. He unbuttoned his suit coat and vest, donned the shop apron, and went to work. Nine Fingers pounded the nails into the wall; Horace handed him the paintings.

"I don't see a single name I recognize," Horace said.

"Glad to hear that," Nine Fingers answered when he took a small nail out of his mouth. "I'll explain it to you over lunch."

"Well, I, ah...," Horace sputtered.

"My treat. If it makes you feel any better, you can stand me the next time – after you get paid. They do a killer whitefish lunch over to the Butler Hotel," Nine Fingers answered. Horace had to turn his back to him to prevent his employer from seeing his smile.

"Whitefish, you say? You're on," Horace said. "Thank you. You don't mind me asking where you find all these artists, do you?"

"No, not at all. I don't know if you've heard of it, but there's a place across the river called Ox-Bow. It's an art school that got started by some art teachers out of Chicago. Before I hung out my shingle I went out there to talk with the students. Most of them were quick to sign up. So, that's why you probably haven't heard of them. Give them time, and you will. Some of them, at least."

Twenty minutes later they locked up the gallery and walked down the street to the hotel.

A good whitefish lunch was the perfect way to end what had become a very good morning, and when the two men shook hands outside on the street, Horace was almost smiling. Not enough of a smile that anyone would notice or think he'd had a bump or two to make him pixilated, but he was purring on the inside.

Then his life got better. Doctor Landis spotted him and pulled over. "I was just coming to see you, Horace. Hop in and I'll explain." Doctor Horace got in the car, half-expecting it to be an emergency, but Landis turned off the engine. "I'll come straight to the point. I need you to work at the hospital in the afternoons. Simple as that. There isn't that much going on, but I want the place covered at least until the middle of September. I need to spend time with the boys before they go back to school, and then catch up on my reading. I really need you. Just afternoons...." His voice trailed off.

"Afternoons? Sure. My mornings are kind of busy, but sure, the rest of August and first couple of weeks of September." He stuck out his right hand and the two men shook on the deal.

Doctor Landis explained he had some spare time and suggested they drive around. "Thought you might like to see that not everyone lives on a boat," he laughed. He did a U-turn on Butler, then turned up Hoffman Street. "Now, that used to be a vacant lot over there until some fellow bought it. Look, they're already building. It's one of those kit homes from Sears. The whole house comes in pieces in a boxcar and they just put the pieces together."

"I'm sure there is a lot more to it than that," Horace said quietly as he looked at the project.

The evening was warm enough to have dinner on the deck of the *Aurora*, and once the dishes were cleared away, everyone was surprised when Horace brightly said, "I want to hear what everyone did today. Adventures, new things, old things, any old thing." He turned to Theo and said, "Little brother, start us off."

Theo and Clarice were caught off guard, and couldn't think of anything interesting to contribute. Nor could Fred. Harriet said a few things about the artists at Ox-Bow, but not much more. "Well, Phoebs, it's up to you and me. Ladies first."

Phoebe looked horrified, swallowed hard, and softly blurted out, "Well, I stopped by the Western Union today, and I got hired as the relief telegrapher." She quickly looked down at her lap, waiting for the grown-ups to respond.

"You did what?" her mother Harriet demanded. "I would have thought you would at least talk it over with me first!"

"Well, there wasn't much time. I was walking past the office and saw the help wanted sign, and I am a good telegrapher, so I went in. And I was hired on the spot. It's just part-time until school starts," Phoebe answered. She didn't add that she would be working on Saturday mornings in the fall.

"I think there is something to be said about her initiative," Clarice said quietly, once again trying to smooth ruffled feathers.

"Yes, but..." Harriet protested.

"Yes, and now she knows the next time to ask first," Clarice smiled.

Before anyone else could speak, Horace quickly changed the subject. "Well, young lady, you're not the only one with a surprise. I ran into a fellow who is new to town and opened an art gallery, and the rum thing is, he hired me on the spot to work for him!"

"Is there a punch line to this joke?" Theo asked.

"No punch line and no joke. His name's Charlie Larsen and...."

"Oh no!" Harriet interrupted. "Please tell me he has all ten of his fingers."

"No, just nine of them. Well now, seven really if you don't count thumbs as fingers, but most people do. His place is called Nine Fingers Charlie's Art Emporium. Why, have you met him?"

Harriet put both hands on the sides of her forehead as if she was fighting a headache. "Yes, I have met him. He's charming and witty and intelligent, but he is undermining how art is sold. What he's doing is underhanded and unfair. It's practically socialism!"

"You want to explain that to me, Harriet?" Horace asked cautiously.

"First of all, the standard split at a gallery is fifty-fifty. Half for the gallery owner; half for the artist. For new artists it's more like sixty percent for the gallery because they're taking a big risk with a newcomer. He's offering an artist seventy-five percent, and worse, a bonus for signing up with him.

"And then second, everyone around here knows that for years Mrs. Comstock has always had the first choice of paintings at Ox-Bow"

"That doesn't sound fair," Horace said, cutting her off.

"Maybe not, but there is good reason for it. She might have just a small gallery here, but she has much bigger ones in Chicago and New York City, oh, and St. Louis. If she takes on an artist then they know they have a future in the best markets. But if this, this, interloper gets in and muddles things up, a good artist could get sidelined right from the start." Harriet explained.

"In other words, they might lose out on a chance to get promoted?" Clarice asked.

"Exactly right," Harriet said. "And you, Horace, are working for him. I'll bet he charmed you like he does everyone else. Well, I can't tell you how to live your life, but my advice is that you walk out on him right now."

"I'll take that under advisement," Horace said flatly, giving no indication of his thoughts.

"Frankly, I simply cannot believe you two. Both of you!" she snapped as she looked at Phoebe and then Horace and back again. Her face was reddening with anger. "I think you've forgotten that I'm your mother and when you want to do something unusual, you need to ask my permission. And you, a surgeon and physician, taking a job for next to nothing at a next to nothing art gallery." She turned to Phoebe, pointed a finger, and said, "Stay here until I return." With that, she stalked across the deck and down to the street.

Clarice put her arm around Phoebe's shoulder. "Don't worry about it. She hasn't caught on to the fact that you're not a little girl any more. Give her some time, and she'll soon tell you how proud she is of you. Trust me, dear!"

In the moment, it was cold comfort to the girl who was shaking and fighting back tears.

"And as for you, Horace, good luck getting yourself out of this kettle of fish," Clarice scolded.

When the others left the table, Fred lingered. "That art shop you're working at sort of sticks in my mind."

"What do you mean?" Horace asked.

"Just the owner's name, that's all. Nine Fingers Charlie. Seems to me that I've heard that name somewhere before, and if I'm right, he was a sort of shady character. He might be on the level, but I'm not so certain. Boss, you may want to watch your back a little."

"Yes, I think you might be right."

"And pardon me for saying it, Boss, but it seems fishy to me that he'd hire a fellow he never met right off the street. I mean, even if it is you he hired, it still seems strange."

"I know. Fred, he never even asked my name. It was almost like he thought we'd been old chums since we were in school. It *is* fishy."

"So, you going to do like Mrs. Harriet wants and quit?"

"Not yet. I want to play this out a bit more."

"Horace, I know you're having a bit of fun with this, and you never were one to miss out on creating a little mischief, but just watch out, would you? If what Fred says pans out, well, just don't get hurt," Theo cautioned him.

"Or anyone else get hurt, either," Clarice added.

THREE

For six delightful days, Doctor Horace, despite the initial bumpiness, revelled in the contentment of a calm and orderly life. Theo and Clarice went off to spend the day strolling from one gallery or shop to the next, playing either bridge or mah-jong, or sipping tea with their friends. On cooler days, they contented themselves by reading under blankets in deck chairs on the *Aurora.* Harriet, after her spat with Phoebe was, exactly as Clarice predicted, very proud of her daughter having her first part time job. She even bragged about her whenever the occasion arose. As for Fred, after years of constantly working for the Balfour Brothers, he enjoyed some time to himself, and even threatened to take painting classes at Ox-Bow, much to Harriet's consternation. Instead, he and Captain Garwood bought a small rowboat so they could fish on the river.

From all appearances, it seemed that Horace was beginning to adjust to the idea of semi-retirement. He enjoyed a quiet early morning, with a new routine of coffee on the deck, a short three-block walk to the store for the papers, and then walking to the gallery to work for Nine Fingers for a few hours. He would come home for lunch and then Fred would take him across the Kalamazoo River to the cottage hospital. "Just don't say anything to him," Theo cautioned his wife one day when they discussed his contentment. "It will most certainly spook him. He might take it as a sign of weakness."

Only Mrs. Garwood knew any different. One morning she spotted the photograph of his late wife on the small table next to his bed. "I knew it," she said to herself. "He is trying to put up a good front." Or, perhaps, she thought, he was trying to convince himself that all was well. Doctor Horace always kept it hidden in the drawer under some papers until he went to bed. For a while he'd moved it to the bureau, completely out of sight and out of mind. Now, it was back to its original spot.

Her lips tightened as she stared at it, debating whether to leave it where it was or discreetly put it away in the drawer. She understood. He was lonely, and hiding from the pain by working two part time jobs.

The sense of peace and stability came to an end mid-morning, just a week after he began working for Nine Fingers. The door was wide open, and two young, smartly and identically dressed twins, walked in. "I'm Maisie and this is my sister Daisy," one of them said.

"No, I'm Maisie, and she's Daisy," the other replied. They both giggled. "We're here to buy art."

"We're here to look at art," the other woman corrected her.

"Well, you've come to the right place. And whichever one of you is which, well, we're just glad you're here, so look around," Nine Fingers answered with a chuckle. And if you have any questions, we're here to help. If you see something you like, we're here to take your money. We'll wrap it up for you for free!"

"Do you take an IOU?" one of them giggled. "We're a little short on money. Ooopsie!"

"We'll discuss that later," Nine Fingers answered cautiously. He looked toward Horace, nodded his head toward the pair, and pulled on his right ear, then mouthed, "Keep an eye on them. Might be light-fingered."

The two of them slowly wandered through the little shop, pretending to look at the art. When Horace pulled out his pipe to fill it, one of them came over and said, "My grandfather smokes a pipe. I just love the smell of a pipe. It makes me go all gooey inside." She was shamelessly flirting. "There is just something about a man and his pipe." She stared up at Horace, making him turn away before she could see his face redden.

Nine Fingers chortled at Horace's discomfort as one of the two women continued, "We're here for a few days. I'll bet you're a man of the world who knows where a girl could buy a little antifreeze, dontcha?"

"Well, I'd try the service station just north of town," Horace answered.

"Ohhhh.... you're funny. That's not the sort of antifreeze I had in mind. You know, a bottle of hootch that makes a girl feel all warm and relaxed."

"Well, ah, ah, I wouldn't know about anything like that. It is against the law, and there's a sharp eyed cop in town," Horace sputtered. "Sorry, I guess I'm not much help." He gulped hard and took a half step back.

She smiled at him and then rejoined her sister for a few minutes. Her twin sister turned toward them and said, "Well, you're no fun. Let's go!"

"We've got to skidoo," Maisie or Daisy said. They walked toward the door, arm in arm, and one of them looked over her shoulder to add, "See you boys in the funny papers!"

Once the two women were down the street Nine Fingers burst out laughing. "Horace, old boy, you turned fourteen shades of red."

As discomforting as Daisy and Maisie had been, it was nothing compared to the next visitors. An older woman marched into the shop. She was tall, stout, expensively dressed in a grey dress, pearls and a summer hat, and wore what was best described as 'sensible shoes.' Following her was a thin elegantly dressed man, also in gray. She had a look of determination on her face, and both men realized this was no social call.

"I demand to speak to the proprietor," she barked.

"That's me. Front and center, Madame. How may I be of service?" Nine Fingers answered.

"I understand your name is Charlie Larsen, although you seem to take some unfortunate child-like delight with your nickname. I am Mrs. Comstock. I am very certain you know of me. I have the Comstock Gallery here in town, as well as galleries in Philadelphia, Chicago, St. Louis, and Manhattan."

Nine Fingers cut her off. "Manhattan, Kansas?" he asked.

"Manhattan in New York City, and in a very prestigious neighbourhood. Why would anyone open a fine art gallery in someplace like Kansas?" Before Nine Fingers could answer, she continued. "I see no reason why you should even be in Saugatuck. You are making a mockery of fine art. Even the name of your so-called gallery is a mockery! If anyone deserves to be in Manhattan, Kansas, it is you. Now, I strongly suggest you contact the artists, tell them to collect their work, pack up, and leave." She looked around the shop and sniffed in derision. "Obviously you are having a hard time making ends meet. I will assist you with the cost of leaving town – immediately!"

Nine Fingers rubbed his chin to stall for time before toying with her. "Well, you see, it's like this. I kinda like Saugatuck. Nice place, and with a couple of exceptions, everyone is real kind. As for needing money, don't you worry your little head about that. I'm more than a little flush."

"Really?" she asked sarcastically. "Then take my advice and just leave!"

Nine Fingers looked at her and said, "No, I think it's you what needs to leave my shop. And take Silent Cal with you. I don't much appreciate riff-raff giving orders, no matter how fancy they dress." He pointed toward the door. "Out! Shoo!" He picked up a push broom for emphasis.

"You haven't heard the last of me!" she snapped.

"I'm pretty sure you're right."

She turned to her husband and commanded him to take her home.

"Don't hurry coming back. Take your time. Lot's of time," he called after them.

"Well, I'd say we just met the infamous Mrs. Comstock and her lap dog. You gotta feel sorry for a mug like him, though. You notice that he didn't even look up, he was so embarrassed?" Nine Fingers sighed. "Well, maybe not. Ashamed, maybe. He was a lawyer for the Illinois Central, as I recall. And there's no one much lower than a railroad lawyer, leastwise not since Lincoln. Railroad lawyers, if you ask me, are worse than Big Al, Rothstein and his gang, and the Dutchman all rolled into one."

"On the whole, I'd rather put up with those Betsy Co-eds rather than Mrs. Curdleface," Horace agreed, giving a slight cough to mask a chortle.

"Say listen, Horace. In another hour or so you've got to change into your white jacket and hang that duma-flaggy thing around your neck. You got people counting on you. What say you knock off a half hour early, go for a walk and forget about that old sourpuss?

And I hate to give advice, but you might enjoy a walk up on the hill. It'll be quiet up there because I doubt those gold diggers will risk their high heals walking that far."

"Appreciate it, Boss," Horace said, his mood lifting. "I think I'll go look at the houses and gardens. Say, why don't you come for dinner? We'll be eating about 6:30 or so, and there's room for another pair of feet under the table."

Nine Fingers nodded. "I don't know about that. I understand your daughter-in-law has her feet planted firmly in Mrs. Comstock's camp. She might not like it if I joined you."

"Don't worry about her. She might be prickly at first, but she'll get over it. You'll see."

Dinner did not go especially well. The moment Harriet realized that it was the infamous Nine Fingers sitting across from her, she bristled, glared, and then averted her eyes, and she remained silent during most of the meal. Finally, after the dishes had been cleared away, she quietly said, "You are making quite a stir of things around here, Mr. Larsen."

"So I've been led to believe, Mrs. Walters," Nine Fingers answered. "That was never my intention. You see, I studied and taught economics, and I am applying some of the principles I believe are essential for progress. I think of it as an experiment."

"And what experiment might that be?" she asked hotly.

"Two things. I believe the split between artist and gallery owner is very uneven. It's even worse in the larger galleries where a sales clerk is given a piece of art in lieu of their normal salary and commission. Now, that usually only happens when a piece sells for a substantial amount of money. I don't think your father-in-law needs to worry about that, at least not for a while."

"They're getting paid for their work," Harriet answered back.

"Yes, but in a way it is deferred payment, and it's not in cash. Let's say they would have earned, what?, two hundred dollars commission, but the gallery owner gives them half or even less of it, and a painting or drawing to square things up. Usually it is something they couldn't sell in the first place. Now, maybe someday the painting will be worth something, or maybe not. My method is different: salary plus commission, and the full commission is in cash. To that end, Doctor Balfour is on straight salary and agreed to a ten per cent commission on everything he sells. So, if he sells a ten dollar painting or one that's worth ten thousand, he gets his full commission."

"That's not how it is done," she fired back.

"Be that as it may. That's how I do it in my gallery."

"Yes, but if the sales clerks at other galleries find out about it, it will create problems. Is there more to your economic theory?"

"Yes, I only work with new artists. I won't touch the works of anyone dead," Nine Fingers answered.

"That's ludicrous! There is no money in new artists. Dead artists pay for the shop and make it possible to introduce new ones. You'll never make any money that way."

"Perhaps not. But, again, it's my shop, my rules, and that's how I'm doing it. I know, it's not traditional, and I don't care. I already got both barrels of that from Mrs. Curdleface Comstock. Now, just relax a bit and let me get on with my economic experiment. Why, you might someday see me win the Nobel Prize for economics."

Harriet chortled. "Curdleface. That's a good name for her. She could make milk curdle while it's still in the cow! Look, all I'm telling you is that you're going to create trouble, and I mean big trouble."

"Yooo-hooo! Hi! Remember us? Maisie and Daisy, remember?" one of the twins giggled as they both waved. "Permission to come aboard, Admiral? Say, someone's got a swell ship."

Horace winced in discomfort as he motioned for them to come up the gangplank.

"Harriet, Fred, Theo and Clarice, Harriet, Phoebs, meet a couple of friends of ours," Nine Fingers Charlie said with a smile.

"This is your ship?" one of them gushed.

"His," Charlie said.

"Say, it's real swell," they answered in unison, then giggled as they looked at each other.

"We're going to the dance at the Big Pavilion. It sure would be swell walking in the door with a couple of real gents like you two. Want to come with us?" one of them asked.

"Right now, that seems like a good idea. It's the best offer so far today," Nine Fingers said. "What do you say, Horace?"

"Well, I, ah, don't know."

Harriet smiled at Horace's discomfort. "Oh, go with them. Live a little."

"Well, I had some other plans for this evening," he protested.

"Yes, I can well imagine. You'll retreat to your study, light your pipe, and read a Sherlock Holmes story you have read a hundred times before. No! Go out, have a good time with these nice *young* ladies."

Horace didn't know what to say.

Harriet would not relent. "Fred, Phoebe, why don't you go along with them? Make a nice party of it." She turned toward her daughter and gave her 'that look' over the top of her glasses. Phoebe's fate was sealed.

"Sure, come along little sister. We'll show you all the latest dance steps," one of them agreed.

"You are absolutely wicked, Harriet," Clarice chided her as they watched the group leave.

"Whatever do you mean?" she asked, trying to sound completely innocent.

"You know very well that Horace will be on his best behaviour if Phoebe is along."

Harriet smiled. "Yes. And they won't stay out very long. In the meantime he'll be squirming in sure embarrassment which is just about what he deserves right now."

"Well done."

FOUR

Harriet's quest for a bit of mischief and revenge failed. Phoebe and Fred came back to the *Aurora* a little before ten o'clock. When she asked him what had become of Horace he shrugged his shoulders and said as far as he knew the boss and Nine Fingers Charlie were still at the Big Pavilion. "Or, maybe they're stepping out with the Gold Dust Twins, for all I know."

"I see," Harriet said, her lips tight.

"Sort of makes you wish Beatrix hadn't gone home so soon," Fred said.

If Harriet agreed, she said nothing. "Well, young lady, time for us to go home and go to bed. You can start practicing going to bed early for when you go back to school."

"Mother...." Phoebe wailed.

"Forward, march!" Harriet said lightly as they walked across the deck. "Left right left right!"

Fred leaned over the rail to watch them walk down Water Street and turn the corner. He counted to ten, then put two fingers in his mouth and whistled. "All clear!" He whistled a second time, waiting until Horace stepped out of the shadows.

"How come you took a powder like that, Boss? I thought you might have enjoyed the company," Fred asked. "Looked to me like you were hitting it off with those two."

"That is *not* my idea of a fun evening. I stayed until you and Phoebe left and came right along behind you," Horace answered.

"Yeah, I saw that. The way I figured it, you didn't want Harriet to figure out you weren't having fun," Fred said. "Course, the fact that you didn't come home with us might just lead her to think you're going to stay up dancing all night till the cows came home."

Horace smiled. "Well, now. If that's what she wants to think, then we'll let her think it."

"You're a regular scamp, Boss," Fred chortled. "Regular scamp."

"Good night, Fred. And let's just leave Harriet to worry about me. It'll take the pressure off of Phoebe."

"Yes, Sir," Fred answered, giving him a salute.

Throughout the mornings the visitors in town, all of them potential customers, filtered in and out of the art gallery. Most of them were merely curious. "Tire-kickers," as Nine Fingers Charlie called them, enticed into the shop by the unusual name. A few of them even asked its origin.

When Nine Fingers Charlie wasn't working with another customer he would give a gentle smile and explain, "Well, it's like this. I lost one of my fingers in an accident so I got the nickname. And when I came here, well, I just used it for my shop." His answer seemed to satisfy them, but for some reason, Horace thought there was more to it than just that.

A few of the customers weren't satisfied with the answer, either, and wanted to know what sort of an accident. Nine Fingers was prepared for them. "Well, back when I was a tyke, my sister dared me to ride on the front of the lawnmower while she pushed it. The blade got in the way of my finger." If it was a young boy he added, "So, let that be a lesson to you."

After the two men had been working together and Horace had had time to size him up, he felt sufficiently comfortable to ask, "Just what sort of an accident did you have?"

"Oh, it was pretty stupid. I lost it in a lawnmower blade. I was sharpening it and I had put a screwdriver to keep the blades from turning. It slipped, the blades moved, and so did my finger."

It seemed reasonable. Horace had seen accidents like that, and far worse, many times. Still, he was curious to know more about his employer.

"What was your line before you came here?" Horace asked one morning as he was sweeping the floor.

"Well, let's see. I studied mathematics and economics at McGill University under Stephen Leacock..."

"Hold on. I thought Leacock is a writer," Horace objected.

"He is now. But long before the war he was just a university professor, and a good one, too. I studied under him and got my degree in economics. After that, I taught at a boy's school in Rhode Island for a few years, and then moved out west to Minnesota to teach at an Episcopal school there. Not too exciting is it? And now I run an art gallery. There you have the gist of it."

Horace was about to ask more when the door came open. "Hi, I'm Daisy! This is my sister Maisie!" one of the two blondes said brightly for the second day in a row.

"No, silly! I'm Daisy and you're Maisie!" her twin answered. Once again they were dressed the same, making it impossible to tell them apart. Horace was almost relieved that they were not wearing the same dresses from the night before.

"Charlie, we had a swell time last night. And you, Horace, you're a party-pooper!" one of them said.

"Party-pooper!" her sister added, sticking out her tongue in mock anger. "You should have stayed. Charlie's a swell dancer, but we had to take turns. Are you a swell dancer too, Horace? We're going to the Big Pavilion again tonight. Why don't you come with us? Please? Pretty Please?"

"And with sugar on it!" the other twin giggled.

Horace's face began to redden, and he quickly looked at his pocket watch, and then told Charlie, "I've got to go over, ah, go over across the street and ah, have some coffee."

Before he could finish one of the two women said, "Oh, we'll go with you, Horace!"

"Ah, no! No! Charlie, I'll see you later." Horace was still pulling on his suit coat as he hurried out the door. Behind him were the stinging giggles of the two women.

The two Flappers were still talking and flirting with Charlie when one of them noticed a car pulling up in front of the store. She interrupted her sister, pointed to it, and then asked, "You have a back door out of here? We need to make tracks, and fast."

Charlie pointed to the back door of the shop, and told them there was no back alley. "Stay put in there and pipe down. I'll give you the all-clear when it's safe again." He watched as they left the show room and pulled the door closed behind them, then turned his attention to the couple coming in the front door.

"Are you still here? Why?" Mrs. Comstock asked in a raised shrill voice. "I thought I made it abundantly clear that there is no place for you in Saugatuck." She looked around the shop and sneered. "No one wants you. Just as I thought, not a customer in sight!"

Standing behind her, silent as the last time, was the well dressed, gray, weary-looking man. He averted his eyes from both Nine Fingers and Mrs. Comstock. Even when Nine Fingers Charlie stared at him, he refused to make eye contact.

"Surely, even someone with your limited intelligence can see that there is no future in remaining here. Cut your losses and leave. Just leave! I will make arrangements with the artists to transfer them to my gallery. And the best of them will know that they will be exhibited in my galleries elsewhere. Well? What is your answer?"

Nine Fingers Charlie rubbed his beard to stall for time. Slowly he began to answer. "You see, I like it here. It's a nice little town, and from what I've seen, most of the people are all right. There are some notable exceptions, of course, present company included. And since I'm not too worried about money, I think I'll stay. I appreciate your offer, but just the same, I'm going to stay. And besides, I don't like the idea of being run out of town, especially by an over-stuffed society dame."

"You haven't heard the last of this!" she shouted at him.

"Now, now that's the first intelligent thing you've said since I met you. I'm pretty certain you'll come back again. People with a screw loose like you stick to a subject like a rat terrier. You ought to see a doctor to get your head screwed on right. Meanwhile, I've got work to do, so unless you're going to put some cash down for a painting, this is a good time to leave. I don't like having my gallery cluttered up." He pointed to the door. "And don't forget to take the sphinx with you. I don't take in strays." He chuckled at her as she became increasingly angry.

Mrs. Comstock pulled herself up to her full height, her shoulders back, and glared in fury. She paused for a few seconds, hoping to intimidate Nine Fingers Charlie, then turned around and left.

"All clear, ladies. Boxcar Bertha and her spook left," he said once the big Cadillac started down the street. "Just how did you run across those two? They don't seem like you're type."

"Oh, it's a long story. Boxcar Bertha and the spook – you've got a way with words, Charlie, you know that? You've got a way with words. That's why we're both so sweet on you. You're a really sweetie, you know that! Too bad you can't get Horace to loosen up a bit. The four of us could have some good times," one of them flirted.

"I think you two ought to clear out of here. No telling whether that old battle-axe is going to come back for a second round. She was pretty hot under the collar, and I doubt she's the type to bottle it up," Nine Fingers Charlie warned them. "You know anything about them? Anything at all?"

"Just that the man is a retired big shot lawyer for the CB&Q," one of them said.

"CB&Q? What's that?" he asked, pretending not to know

"Chicago Burlington and Quincy Railroad. I'll bet he is loaded," she giggled. "Are you loaded?"

Nine Fingers pointed toward the door, nodded, and flashed a quick smile as they left.

"Didn't think I'd be seeing you again so soon," Nine Fingers Charlie said as Horace returned to the gallery.

"Oh, I just went out for a cup of coffee," he replied. "Say, I overheard one of the women say that Mr. Comstock worked for the CB&Q. I thought you said he worked for the Illinois Central."

"Ah, who knows. One railroad lawyer is as crooked as the next one," Nine Fingers Charlie said with a wave of his hand. "And now that all our guests are gone I guess you thought you'd come back to keep me company," he laughed. "Not that I can blame you about

Madame Curdlepuss. She's a real piece of work. Now, those two nice young ladies, they're another story. Now, what say you join us at the Big Pavilion tonight, and this time stay for a while. You know who's playing tonight, don't you? It's Miff Mole and his organization. Now, if you like trombone music, you'll appreciate Miff. And the girls and I would appreciate it if you're there."

"Tell you what, if I can get away from my family, I'll be there," Horace promised.

"I'm not taking odds on that," Nine Fingers laughed.

"You aren't really going out again tonight with those two Flappers, are you?" Harriet asked.

Before Horace could answer Phoebe asked, "Can I come along with you, Grandfather? Those two ladies are swell."

Horace and Harriet answered in unison: "No!"

"Are you really going out again tonight?" Harriet repeated.

"I don't see why not. I had a perfectly fine time last night. You should hear that Miff Mole on the trombone! I think he's aces. Now, I need to freshen up and get ready for a late night. And say, don't wait up for me! Twenty-three skidoo and toodle do, too."

Phoebe watched until her grandfather had gone to his cabin. "I'm getting worried about him," she whispered to her mother.

"You and me, both," her mother said softly.

"It's too bad Beatrix...."

"That will do," Harriet cautioned her. "Why don't you see if Fred will take you out for another driving lesson? I think I'm going home, so please ask Fred to drop you off there when you get back."

Phoebe was driving her grandfather's car on the Holland road when Fred said, "Now, you're getting real good at driving, but there's a trick you ought to learn in case you ever find yourself in a real tight jam and need to make a run for it. You know, if you ever get a boy who's trying to get fresh on you and right on your back bumper. I'm the one to teach it to you."

Phoebe looked straight ahead, trying not to let Fred see her smile. She listened as he explained, "Now, you see, it's called a bootleggers term on account of the fact that sometimes if Johnny Law is getting too close and they need to make a getaway, they use it."

As calmly as possible Phoebe asked, "You mean like this?" as she accelerated.

She pressed hard on the clutch, took the gear shift firmly in her right hand, slammed on the brakes and turned the wheel hard to the left, then released the brake. The car spun half way around, and instantly she shifted back into high gear and pressed down on the accelerator. Fred's face drained of color and he was holding tightly to the door. Before he could say anything, Phoebe said smugly, "Beatrix already taught me that."

"Well, good, I guess. Yes, that's a good thing, all right. You got the basics down pat, but you could have told me you were going to do it," Fred sputtered. "And you ought to practice more, too."

"Should we do it again?" she asked.

"No, no, no, I think once a night is enough. Yeah, for sure, once a night is enough," he told her. "And you listen to me, young lady, you save that turn for a real emergency. I don't want you doing that to show off. It's dangerous even if you know what you're doing. You understand me?" Fred cautioned.

"Loud and clear, Sergeant," she promised.

FIVE

"Well, I might have known you'd turn up," Chief Garrison growled at Doctor Horace as he walked toward the art gallery. With the chief was another, very young, patrolman.

"You're right. I work here," Horace answered breezily. "I take it you're looking to buy a painting for your office. You know, pretty it up a little."

"You work here? Then why don't you tell me why there's a dead body on the floor and the door is locked and no one's around? You selling dead bodies, now?" The chief demanded, "You got a key?"

"What? What body? What are you talking about? And no, like I said, I just work here. Charlie, Charles, I assume, Larsen, owns the gallery. He's got the key, not me."

"I got a call from someone who looked in the window and he said there was a body in here. I want to know what's going on. And just where does this Mr. Larsen live?" the chief demanded.

"I think he has a couple of rooms over the shop, but I don't know that for sure. I've never been up there."

"Well, no-never mind. That door is locked and I need to get in there to see what's what!" the chief demanded.

"Before you break the door down and get glass all over the crime scene, if there even is one, let me see if I can get in," Horace offered. He reached for a small leather case in his jacket pocket. "Medical tools. Actually, they're dental tools. A dentist down in Chicago by the name of Dr. Runyon gave them to me. Sometimes they can be used for other things," he explained.

"Be that as it may; it seems awfully queer that you being a doctor is so good at picking locks," Garrison snarled.

"We all have our little hobbies, don't we?" Horace concentrated on working the two small metal tools, one a rod, the other a serrated bar, slipping them into the key hole before twisting them until he heard the satisfactory snap of the opened lock. "All yours," he said, stepping to one side so the chief could enter the dark gallery.

"Well, let's see who we've got," the chief said, glancing at a patrolman to be sure he was taking notes.

He rolled the body onto her back. "Holy moley! That's Mrs. Comstock!"

"I believe we can ascertain the cause of death," Horace said softly. "Bullet in the heart. From the looks of the wound, a small calibre. Instantaneous death."

"I got eyes. I can see it. And we didn't even need your lady doctor friend to tell us how she died. Now, where is that Mr. Larsen?" He looked at his officer and ordered him to go upstairs and bring him down immediately. Horace and the chief heard him thud up the stairs, a door opening and closing, and him returning to the main floor.

"Nobody up there, and it doesn't look like he spent the night in his bed," the young officer said.

"Well, that just about settles it in my mind. Dead woman on the floor, shot through the heart, and the owner of the business is on the run." The chief stood up and reached out to shake hands with Horace. "Well, thank you for your time, but this is an open and closed case. You're dismissed." He chortled at his statement. "Looks like you opened the door and I closed the case!" He pointed toward the door and ordered Horace to leave.

"I think a little more investigation is in....."

"I said you're dismissed. I want you off the premises. Now!"

"...order," Horace completed his sentence, "and an autopsy."

"Yes, yes, yes. Doctor Landis will be doing the autopsy, and without your help. You're too close to this murder. Now, off the premises or I'll have you run in for interfering with an official police investigation."

Horace shrugged his shoulders in disgust and walked out the door. His morning routine had been thrown off, and it made him uncomfortable, to say nothing of a shocking murder and his boss implicated. He was uncertain what he should do. Going back to the boat didn't seem like a good plan because he would only be peppered with questions by a half-awake Theo. Fred would become excited and want to get them involved, and for some reason, this time Horace had no desire to get involved in a murder. There was no point in going to the hospital when Doctor Landis would soon be busy with an autopsy. That left a visit to the diner for coffee, scrambled eggs, bacon, and toast. Horace ruled out that idea because there would be too many people who would want to know what happened at the art gallery.

With his pipe leaving a trail of smoke behind him, he walked toward the park, stopping to buy a Chicago newspaper, so that he could hide behind it as he sat on a bench. The contents were not really of any interest to him; he wanted the time and privacy to think.

It was not surprising that Chief Garrison announced he had already solved the crime. A dead woman in the shop and the owner missing made a good probable cause and connection. It was simple and the easiest conclusion. "All I have to do is find the killer and lock him up," he boasted to his officers. "And I already know who he is," he added in triumph. It was the crime itself that made no sense, and Horace repeated his own dictum to himself, "Murder always makes sense, if only to the person who did it." So far, the answers were not apparent.

Horace flinched slightly when he realized someone had sat down next to him. "Fred, how did you find me?" he asked.

"Small town so it isn't too hard. And then when I heard about that business over to the art shop I figured you'd wander off to be alone. All I had to do was follow my nose." When he realized Horace looked confused, Fred added, "Your pipe."

"It doesn't make sense, Fred," Horace said quietly after he folded up his newspaper. "Nine Fingers Charlie has the only key, at least that I know of, so how did Mrs. Comstock get in, and who shot her? There was no gun around, so that rules out suicide. And from what I could see in Nine Fingers Charlie, he wasn't the sort of man to carry a gun, much less use it.."

"Now, you might want to slow down on that one, Boss. Maybe he was feeding you a line about his past. Maybe he wasn't all he seems to be."

"You might be right about that," Horace agreed with reluctance.

"Meanwhile, what's got me jumpy is that Garrison is likely going to want to have a long talk with you, and he's not going to be happy if you don't have some answers, the right answers, for him," Fred said.

Horace emptied out his pipe, tapped it against the sole of his left shoe a few times, and almost immediately refilled it. "You're probably right," he finally answered. He shook the match out and added, "I'd better let Theo know what's happened."

"Doc, maybe it isn't my place to be saying this, and maybe it is, but this just might be an old fashioned case of simple murder. Don't you always say the simple answer is usually the right one? Well, the way I look at it, maybe that's what we have here. Nine Fingers Charlie plugged the woman and then ran off."

Horace didn't answer as he stood up and walked back to the boat, Fred walking next to him.

Theo and Clarice had already finished their breakfast and gone off for the morning. If they hadn't already heard about the late Mrs. Comstock's body in Nine Fingers Charlie's art gallery, they soon would. Waiting on deck of the *Aurora* for Horace was Chief Garrison.

"We took finger prints of that store, and I got to tell you, my guess is we'll your prints are all over the place," Garrison said firmly. "I want you over to the station right away so we can take your prints, you hear me?"

"Considering the fact that I've been working there for over a week, that doesn't surprise me all that much. Shouldn't surprise you, either. You'll find mine, Nine Fingers Charlie, and maybe some customer's left their prints around, too. No telling how many."

"Well, the way I look at it, this Nine Fingers Charlie fellow must have done the old girl in, but I'm not ruling out any suspects just yet. That includes you!

"Now, I just got back from seeing Dr. Landis, and just like I knew right from the get-go the victim was killed with a single bullet straight through the heart. He told me you're working part time with him, and now that the autopsy is over there's no reason you can't keep on doing what you're doing. Once I get your prints, that is. I can't figure out why a man at your age and with all your money cares about working, but you've always been an odd one."

"What about the gallery?" Horace asked.

"That's a closed up crime scene and until I say so, it's staying closed. If I'm right about things, then it's going to be permanently closed once I get that Nine Fingers Charlie locked up! You'll keep out of there along with everyone else!"

"Slow down a second, Chief. I see what you're doing, but there's something else to consider. All of those paintings in there are on consignment. Shouldn't the artists be allowed to collect their work so they can sell them elsewhere?"

Garrison looked at Doctor Horace with disgust. "I don't care if Mozart himself has a painting in there. That place is locked up tight until I say so!"

Horace knew that he was talking with a hot-headed idiot, and decided not to say anything more than, especially about Mozart being a composer and not a painter. "That's your business, but it won't be good for publicity."

"Well, I've said my piece, and we both know where I stand, and what I say is what goes around here!" the chief said as he stood up. "I'm going to call you in for a lot of questions, so don't go any-wheres out of town, you hear?"

Horace didn't answer, and sat mutely as he and Fred watched the police chief leave the *Aurora*. "Fingerprints! Now!" the chief shouted from the sidewalk.

"I didn't know Mozart was a painter," Fred said.

"He wasn't. Look, as long as you're sitting here, drive me over to Dr. Landis' office, would you?" Horace asked. "I'd like you to wait for me. This shouldn't take too long."

"The chief wants to take your prints, Doc," Fred said.

"I heard him. He can wait. I want to talk with Dr. Landis first."

"I hear you've had a busy morning," Horace said with a slight smile as he walked into Dr. Landis' office.

"You mean Mrs. Comstock? Yeah. The autopsy was simple enough. It was a single bullet through the heart and instantaneous death. There are a lot of worse ways to go, as we both know. Now look, Horace, I've got to step down the hall for a moment, and I know you're not supposed to go looking into the case, but I also know you're the curious type. Just in case you want to snoop, before you mess up my paperwork, the file is on the top of the pile on the left corner of my desk." Landis rubbed his left index finger across his nose.

"A pile for everything, and everything in its pile," Horace teased. "You ever think about tidying this office up a little?"

"Nah, not really. It took a long time and a lot of work to get it looking like this," Dr. Landis laughed as he left the room.

"You were right about it being as straight forward as it comes," Horace said, nodding toward the autopsy file when his friend returned a few minutes later.

"Say, I was just thinking. With you having your mornings empty, how about you working here full time the rest of the week so I can take the family up north? The wife would like to get out of town, and with school starting...." Dr. Landis suggested.

"Well, nothing better to do at the moment, at least," Horace said quietly. With the gallery closed, and now that Phoebe had a part time job, he had nothing on his calendar except boredom.

"Day after tomorrow then?" Doctor Landis asked. "And look, Horace, this isn't chiselled in stone yet. I've got to run it past the wife."

"That's always a safe thing to do," he answered. "Say, what about this afternoon?"

Doctor Landis waved him off. "Take a look at all these papers. I need to spend some time cleaning things up. Go and have some fun."

Horace's face dropped when he left the office. Fun? He had no idea what to do that might be fun. "Fred, let's drive around a bit before we go back to the *Aurora*."

"Right have your fingerprinting, Boss," Fred said firmly.

SIX

The murder of Mrs. Comstock took top billing in the local conversation and gossip. Everyone knew she was dead, of course, and no one liked the fact that she had been murdered in cold blood. They liked the idea of a killer on the loose even less. As to whether it was a good or bad thing that Mrs. Comstock was no longer around was another matter. She was a business owner who had supported the local arts, but she was a tough and unpleasant woman who didn't hesitate to use her money and force of personality to get her way. Even a few of her regular customers didn't like dealing with her. Still, no one was wearing a black arm band in mourning.

For an hour or so Horace sat at a window table in the little restaurant across the street from Nine Finger's art gallery, watching people slow down as they walked past the shop. Some of the more curious paused to look through the window, cupping their hands around the sides of their head to get a better view of what was inside. Not that there was much to see. The shop was dark and nothing had changed since Chief Garrison authorized the removal of her body. A mother and her young son picked up their pace to hurry past, as if there might be another shooting at any moment.

"So, what do you think happened?" Melba Root, the waitress, asked as she brought more coffee. "Liver and onions again today?"

"No idea. None at all. All I know is that Mrs. Comstock's body was found on the floor," Horace answered. "And yes to the blue plate special."

"Well," Melba said softly, looking around to make sure no one was listening, "I heard that she took a bullet through the heart. And, I heard that the fellow who owns the place is on the run, and that Chief Garrison got the governor to have the State Patrol out looking for him. And, I heard there is a big reward for whoever brings him in dead or alive!"

"Now, where did you hear that?" Horace asked.

"I got it from Jake who brings in the produce from the store who got it from the fellow who brings down the butter and milk from Holland," she said with a satisfying nod.

"I wonder where the milkman heard it?" Horace asked.

"Well!" Mabel retorted, "I'm sure he got it from official sources. People just don't make up stuff like that, you know!" She turned on her heels and stalked off, miffed that Doctor Balfour would challenge her.

Horace finished his coffee and lunch just as Theo walked past the window, saw him and paused, then came into the cafe. "I thought I might find you here," he said as he sat down. "Anything special happening?"

"No, unless it's that the liver wasn't made into a burnt offering today. At least not yet, or maybe something did before I got here. Or, maybe something will happen a minute after I leave. I'm just watching people stop by the scene of the crime," Horace replied.

"I'm sure there is a good reason for that," Theo answered.

"I don't know that there is. Most people walk past, mostly tourists I'd say, who don't know about the murder or don't care. Some of them slow down but when they see the door is locked, they move on. Some of the locals slow down and look in, and then move on, too. Interesting hobby, this people watching."

"Any of them come around a second time?" Theo asked.

"No. Well, the cashier at Fruitgrowers bank came by twice, but he was walking in a hurry like he was on an errand. Oh, and Bobbie from the switchboard came past twice, pretending she was on an errand, but I'm pretty sure she was just curious. Oh, and a few kids who haven't got anything better to do. That's what I've been watching for, but so far, nothing." He picked up his empty coffee cup, looked at it, and said, "Anyway, I was about to leave. Well, if you want a cup....?" he asked.

"No. I'm fine. Thanks for asking. You going back to the boat?" Theo asked.

"Might as well. Landis doesn't want me underfoot today so he can clear off some paper work," Horace said quietly. He's talking about going away for a few days and wanted to know if I'd like to fill in. We'll see what happens. Theo knew he was bored and didn't know what to do with himself.

"Horace, it's a bit disappointing, isn't it?" Theo asked.

"What?"

"Well, you know, not much of a challenge this time. There doesn't look like there is anything to solve other than finding Nine Fingers Charlie and taking down his confession. Come on, spill it. You know it's disappointing, especially when you like solving a mystery."

Horace didn't answer.

Horace's boredom was short-lived. Right after lunch, after Phoebe had rushed off to the Western Union office and Theo and Clarice had asked Fred to drive them to the beach, Horace took up residence in a deck chair to start reading a new book. He thought he had pulled a mystery off a shelf in his office, but it was a light comic novel. If he wasn't already comfortable in his chair he might have taken it back, but he found a book mark between a couple of the pages. "You could use a change," it read, and he recognized the note was in Beatrix's hand. Horace flinched at the coincidence and truth – he could use a change. Within a couple of pages he was so captivated by some silly London fellow named Bertie and his valet Jeeves he didn't notice that Chief Garrison was coming up the gangplank.

"I need to talk with you, Balfour!" the chief roared.

Horace put down his book, looked at him and said, "Generally, people ask permission to come aboard. And, most younger gentlemen of your age address me as 'Doctor Balfour.'"

"I don't need your permission to come aboard. I'm here on official police business, and by rights I could haul you in to my office right now, if it wasn't so musty smelling thanks to you and the fire department. Your office – now!" He walked across the deck and opened the door to Horace's library, waiting for him to step inside. Horace moved quickly, sitting in his chair behind his desk before the chief could get to it first.

"Have a seat," Horace offered. The chief stared at him, looked down at the chair in confusion, and finally sat down.

"Now, I want to know what you know, and I mean I want you to spill all the beans, about this Nine Fingers Charlie and his painting shop." The chief pulled out a small notebook.

"I don't know very much, really," Horace said. "I was walking past his place one day and saw he'd just opened, so I stopped in. Next thing I know he offered me a job."

"A job? Just like that? A perfect stranger, hired right off the street. Now, fill in the missing pieces!"

"Thanks for the compliment. I never thought of myself as perfect," Horace said cheerfully. "That's the whole story. He said he needed someone to work part time, and he offered me the position."

"And you took it, just like that? Come on. Nobody does that. And you, especially you're a world famous doctor and saw-bones working for a few cents an hour. I'm not buying that!" the chief shouted. "I don't know who's the bigger fool – him for hiring you like that or you for taking the job. It ever cross your mind that maybe he set you up as a cover or something?"

"It doesn't really matter if you are buying it or not. That's what happened, and that's the end of the story." Horace reached for his pipe. "He's an odd duck, that's for sure, but he seemed nice enough from the start. And when it comes to artists, well...."

Garrison glared at Horace. "You ought to know all about that," he sneered.

"That's the way it is sometimes, Chief."

"So, you're sticking to this story you went to work for a fellow and you didn't know anything about him? That's a bit farfetched, and you know it! Where did he come from? Who's his people? Where'd he come up with the money to open an art shop? Start talking, would you?"

"All right. Now, if that's what you want to know, I got something for you. He said he got a degree in economics and he taught math at a boy's school out east, and then another one in Minnesota. Shattuck Hall in Faribault, maybe, probably. He said it was an Episcopal school and that's the only one I know of out there. Then again, I didn't look into it. And then he said that he'd read a lot of John Ruskin's ideas about buying new art, and that's what he was trying to do. Not buy, but just sell. He'd only sell new art from new artists," Horace explained.

"Yeah? And how'd he do? "

"Well, I really don't know. I wasn't there all that long."

"And you know that he and Mrs. Comstock weren't exactly the best of friends, and then she ends up dead on the floor of his place, and he ends up missing."

"So it seems," Horace said, filling his pipe and lighting it, filling his library with thick smoke that made the chief cough.

"Tell me about the beef he and this Mrs. Comstock had," the chief demanded.

"I don't know anything about what they ate," Horace said firmly.

"Now you're acting like a wise guy. That's not the type of beef I meant, and you know it. Don't get cutesy with me. They had a dust up, and at least a couple of times from what I heard. What about?"

"Well, from what I overheard, and what I learned from my daughter-in-law, Mrs. Walters, Nine Fingers Charlie was over-paying what Mrs. Comstock paid on commissions paid to artists, and she didn't like it. I hear the going rate is usually fifty-fifty, but he was offering seventy five-twenty five. She didn't like it."

"So, Nine Fingers Charlie puts a bullet through her heart over, what, a few dollars? That's a bunch of pixie dust, if you ask me. Pure hooey. It doesn't make sense."

"I wouldn't know," Horace said, taking a long puff on his pipe.

"And you wouldn't happen to know where this Nine Fingers fellow comes from?"

"No. We never got around to that."

"So you don't know where he might have gone, either, do you?"

"No, again," Horace said.

"Which means if I was to have a little look-see around your boat, I wouldn't find him hiding out here, would I?" the chief threatened.

"Be my guest, but bring back a search warrant with you. Now, if you haven't got anything else to ask me, I'm reading a fascinating book about Lord someone or the other who's got a castle in England and raises pigs." Horace stood up and nodded toward the door. He smiled slightly, hearing the sound of footsteps hurrying past the library.

The answer provoked Chief Garrison. He stomped out of the room and followed Horace across the deck. "You're slipping into your second childhood, and you don't know it. Some English lord who has a castle and is a pig farmer! Who in their right mind would read such a book?" The chief started down the gangplank to the street. "I'll be back with a warrant to search this boat. You're holding out on me, Dr. Balfour!" Several people passing by turned to look at him, then up to the boat railing and back at Horace.

"Mrs. G, if that is lemonade you're offering, I'd appreciate it if you used a clean glass," he said with a smile. "Caught you, didn't I?" She was coming around the corner from behind his study.

"It's a housekeeper's solemn duty to look after the well-being of her employer. I wasn't eaves dropping, just making sure you were all right," she sputtered as she blushed.

"And isn't it a good thing I never had Captain Garwood repair that bullet hole in the wall. I kept it as a memento, but it makes it easier to hear, doesn't it, especially with a drinking glass right over it?"

Mrs. Garwood stamped her left foot in frustration and moved quickly into the kitchen, then turned around and said, "And if you want lemonade, go get me some lemons!"

SEVEN

For what should have been a drowsy late summer mid-week afternoon, there was a sudden downpour of activity in Saugatuck. Tourists who had seen the police chief's car next to the *Aurora* were quick to pool their ignorance as they speculated as to its meaning. Their speculation infected a few others. A little later, when they over-heard the final shouted threats from Chief Garrison, the whole matter seemed to take on more seriousness. It was the new topic of discussion at the cafes and on the park benches.

To make matters a bit more interesting, Chief Garrison's next stop was the Western Union office. He parked in front of the building and strode in. When he spotted Phoebe and instantly recognized her as Doctor Balfour's granddaughter his attitude was even more surly. "Your boss in?" he demanded without any pleasantry. She said he was in the back office, and he snapped, "Get him." When Mr. Higgins came through the door Chief Garrison looked at Phoebe and said, "Go take a hike. Get yourself an ice cream soda or something and don't come back for half an hour."

Phoebe looked at her employer and was only partially re-assured when he slightly nodded his head that it was all right for her to leave.

"Pad," the chief said firmly, pointing to the yellow paper. He spent a couple of minutes carefully printing out a message, then pushed the paper back to the telegrapher. "Send it, and give me the paper back." The Western Union man did as he was told, watching as the chief pulled the paper off the pad, folded it up, and put it in his pocket. "If you know what's smart, you'll keep your mouth shut, especially around that girl."

Phoebe had watched the office from across the street, waiting until Chief Garrison walked out the front door and closed it hard behind him. She wandered down the block a little, looking in the windows, and then took her time walking back to work.

"Just don't ask any questions," Mr. Higgins said sadly. "It has nothing to do with you." He paused and gently smiled. "Nor your grandfather." Phoebe just nodded. The moment he wandered back into his office and closed the door, she picked up the message pad and tore off the top few pages, folded them, and tucked them into the top of her stocking.

After Horace's unpleasant time with the chief, he was so prickly and restless that he went for a walk. That in itself was not surprising because it was his usual method of sorting out a problem; not telling Mrs. Garwood or someone on the *Aurora* that he was leaving was unusual. Mrs. Garwood watched him go down the gangplank, her lips tightening as she saw his straw boater was not jauntily tilted to one side. "He's not in a good mood," she told herself.

"The boss must have something on his mind," Fred wryly commented when he saw Mrs. Garrison watching him walk down the sidewalk. Her eyes widened, and she motioned him to come into the ship's galley. For the next few minutes she told him everything she had over-heard between Doctor Horace and the police chief.

"You're sure you heard it right?" Fred asked. "Even the police chief isn't so stupid as to think Doc might have had something to do with that woman's murder."

"I'm telling you, the chief came storming up here saying how he ought to be hauling Doctor Balfour off to jail right then and there!"

"That man is nuttier than your fruitcake at Christmastime!" Fred said. "The idea of him saying those things. Now, does your man know about any of this? Or anyone else?"

"Nobody, least not from me. You're the first person I've seen since the chief was here. I'm sure Doctor Horace won't be talking about it."

"Good. Let's keep it that way. Say nothing to Doctor Theo and his missus or your man, either. And we sure got to keep quiet about it around Phoebe, poor girl," Fred told her. "Keep quiet, listen, and think. That's what we've got to do for right now!"

"Knowing how people talk, it won't be long before the whole town hears about it," Mrs. Garwood said sadly.

Fred didn't answer, but he was certain a lot of people already knew and were talking. "I'd better guard his rear in case someone tries slipping up on him," he muttered as he started for the gangplank.

"And so he doesn't do something he'll regret later," Mrs. Garwood muttered to herself.

"I hear you've had ah, ah, an interesting day," Theo said quietly as he sat down in the leather arm chair in his brother's study late that afternoon. He looked at his watch; there was sufficient time before dinner for them to talk.

"I'd say so, yes," Horace answered quietly.

"A very interesting day, the way I hear tell."

"You're probably right," he said flatly.

"And what are you doing about it?" Theo asked.

Horace didn't answer.

Theo was uncomfortable with his brother's silence and blank stare. "Look, we've both been in tough situations before, going all the way back to the day we hung out our shingle, and it never gets much easier," he began. He saw Horace about to say something and held up a hand to stop him. "This has been a tough year. We got pushed out of our own practice, the Chicago boys got the best of us after we nailed that golfer's killer, Beatrix left earlier than you wanted, and now this mess with Mrs. Comstock and Nine Fingers Charlie. Anything you want to add to it?"

"No, I'd say that about covers it."

"Not quite. You're miserable because Phoebe is growing up, too, and you know it," Theo added. "It's not like when you first met her."

"Like you said, it's not been an easy year of it. And the future looks pretty murky, if you want my opinion," Horace said softly.

"And I'll tell you another thing. You went to work for this Nine Fingers Charlie and you thought he was an all right sort of fellow. A bit of a bohemian in some ways, and let's face it, you certainly are not. But he had a brain and knew how to use it, which you admire. And from what I've heard, he had all the charm you don't have. Then this Mrs. Comstock is found dead on his floor and he's missing, and what's got you more anxious than a long tailed cat in a room full of electric fans is that he just really might be a cold blooded killer. You are becoming an ostrich and think if you keep your head in the sand long enough this whole thing will blow over and everything will be just swell again. Well, you're wrong! And re-reading Sherlock Holmes and that new fellow, PG Wodehouse, isn't going to accomplish anything. You might as well pick up that new time-waster called crossword puzzles."

Horace stared blankly at his brother, then slowly nodded in agreement.

"After dinner, let's you and me go for a walk and figure out how we're going to solve this mystery. Let's put our minds together – same as we've always done," Theo suggested.

"Agreed," Horace said, smiling for perhaps the first time that afternoon.

After dinner Theo reminded his brother that they were going for a walk. "Mighty fine dinner, Mrs. G, but we've got to walk off a few of those calories," he announced.

As soon as the others were away from the table, Fred slipped into the galley. "Make you an offer Mrs. G," Fred said.

She cocked her head back to look at him, her lips pursed, wondering what he was about to ask her to do.

"I'll do up these here dishes while you're gone, and as long as you're out, how abouts you finding Doc Horace's address book and jotting down how I can get hold of Doctor Howell?" he asked.

"Fred, I think that's just plain dangerous," she said quietly. "He'll be livid if he finds out!"

"It is and he will, and that's why I'm not doing anything about it just yet. Now, if and when the time should come, and I'm not saying that it will, and I'm not saying that it won't, but if it should come, then it might be helpful to have that information handy-like instead of going on a goose chase searching for it, that is if you get my drift."

"I do." She threw the dishcloth at him. "Get to work."

Over half an hour had passed since Mrs. Garwood left the galley. "Thought you said you knew where he kept informative stuff," Fred objected.

"Oh, I did. I just didn't promise to come running back here. Besides, if you got the paper wet then you might not be able to read it. I figured if I took my time, put my feet up for a few minutes, you'd be done by the time I got back, and I guess I'm about right." She handed him the little square of paper. "I still don't think this is a good idea."

"Me neither, least-wise not right now. Say, where'd you find it."

"That's for me to know and you not to find out."

Knowing that her grandfather and uncle were out for a walk, Phoebe took advantage of the opportunity to slip into Doctor Horace's study to find a lead pencil. She pulled the pages from telegram pad out of the top of her stocking and smoothed it out on the desk. Then, very carefully, and very lightly, she began rubbing the lead over the paper. Gradually, the message appeared, and she read it thoroughly a couple of times.

Phoebe gasped, quickly folded the paper into a small square and tucked it back into her stocking. "Bye Mother, see you at home! Gotta practice my piano!" she shouted as she got about half way down the gangplank. She didn't wait for an answer. She had a stop to make, and still had to get home, catch her breath, and be at her piano bench before her mother returned.

"Bobbie, I need some help – a number and address in Minneapolis, Minnesota. Or it might be in St. Paul!" Phoebe told the town operator.

"I'll do my best, but I don't think I'll have it until morning. Meanwhile, I'll give you some advice to think about and then you can give me your answer when you come back here in the morning. Now, why did you go off to the Western Union when I would have trained you to be a switchboard operator? Dear, don't you realize the world is always going to need switchboard operators, and one of these days the telegram will be completely forgotten. Switchboarding – that's a woman's career to get her into the future. Switchboard or work your fingers to the bone at a typewriter, and nothing will ever replace the good old switchboard!"

Phoebe didn't say anything for a few seconds.

"Besides, you become a switchboard operator, you can learn all sorts of interesting news," Bobbie added.

"Why don't I think Landis is on deck for a social call? Theo asked, nodding toward the town doctor leaning against the rail. He pulled out his pocket watch, looked at it, and added, "Yup, definitely after visiting hours."

"Probably something about me working for him," Horace said. "Let's go up and find out, shall we?"

"Horace, I'll give it to you straight and no chaser. I know you had nothing to do with the murder of Mrs. Comstock. Not a thing. You know it, your family knows it, and I know it. The rum thing is, it's the talk of the town, and it's distracting. I know you won't like this, but, well, I need you to stand down for a few days until the wind changes. Just until then. Look, I talked this over with my missus, and we'll postpone our vacation for a week, and by then everything will be much better. That's when I'll need you," Doctor Landis smiled. "Besides, I've never known you to need much time to tie up a murder case."

"I understand," Horace said quietly. "Theo and I probably would be doing the same thing if the situation were reversed."

"Good. Thank you for understanding. Now, keep me in the picture on what's developing, and don't hesitate to ask if there is anything I can do. Thank you, again, for understanding."

The three men shook hands before Landis returned home. Horace and Theo watched from the rail. "Well, that gives me more free time to solve the murder," Horace said quietly. "And there isn't much to solve."

EIGHT

"Thunderation! You fellows slept in late this morning," Horace called across the deck when he spotted Fred and Theo carrying their coffee toward the table.

"Watch out, he's back to his old self again," Theo whispered.

"Bet it's coffee and that royal jelly Doctor Howell made up for him," Fred whispered back.

Horace waved them toward the chairs. From the number of burnt matches in an ash tray, it was obvious that he had been up for hours. "I have been studying this situation. We have several tasks. The first is put a stop to this nonsense that I'm somehow involved in Mrs. Comstock's murder. The only way to do that is to find out who really did kill her. So, that's the second job. And the third is to find out what's become of Nine Fingers Charlie. Whether he did it, one way or another, we need to find him. Find him and we put this whole mess to an end!" Horace pounded his fist on the table for emphasis.

"And let me take a guess, big brother, you have a plan," Theo said.

"Plan of attack! That's what we need to do – the big push all over again, just like Pershing!" Fred said with enthusiasm.

"That'll do, Sergeant," Horace said.

"You do have a plan to go with this pipe dream, don't you?" Theo asked again.

"I do, and assignments for all. Fred, please start making the rounds of the barbershop, coffee places, and anywhere else you see some of the regulars. Oh, and try the service stations as well, and see if Nine Fingers Charlie stopped to fill up."

"Yes, sir, General!"

"Just keep your ears open and ask a few questions to get the fellows to loosen their lips. Nothing more than that. Don't give them anything more to talk about, is that clear?"

"Yes, sir! No point in letting the enemy know what we're planning. Say, this is like the time we were back in France and...."

Horace cut him off. "We'll tell war stories at the victory celebration. Now, Theo, I'd like you and Clarice to hobnob with some of those society women here in town. You know, the ones who play bridge and that Chinese game, Mah-jong or something, and do those cross-word puzzles to fill up their time, drink a lot of tea, and things like that. Find out what they know about Mrs. Comstock. And, for that matter, her husband, as well."

"And what are you going to do?" Theo asked.

"First thing I'm doing is going out to Ox-Bow to have a look-see and talk with some of the artists out there. They'll talk to me, especially the ones who have their paintings under lock and key. I'll see if I can get the low-down on Nine Fingers Charlie while I'm there," Horace told them.

"Anything else?" Theo asked with a twinge of sarcasm.

"Not yet. Let's see where this leads us first, and then we'll see. Fred, when you're ready, I'd like you to drive me out to Ox-Bow," Horace said. He stood up to put on his suit jacket.

"You want me to wait for you, Boss?"

"No, I don't think so. I don't know if I'm going to be a few minutes or a couple of hours, and I'd like you to get on with your assignment. I'll either get a ride back or walk down the hill and take the chain ferry back."

"I figured you might be done with the chain ferry after what just happened there," Theo suggested. "Say, listen, it's a nice morning and Clarice isn't up yet. I might ride out and back with you."

After they dropped Horace off in front of the Old Inn and watched him enter, Theo asked Fred, "Well, what's your take on this? Something's different this time, if you ask me."

"I think you're right about that, Doc. The boss has got his old energy back, but something doesn't feel right. It's like he's surrounded and besieged from all sides. It's got me a little jumpy. You suppose it might have something to do about Doc Howell not being here?

"Yeah, well, let's get back to town and get started on our assignments."

Horace strolled into the dining hall, looked around, and picked up a knife to wrap against a coffee mug. "Ladies, gentlemen, my apologies for interrupting your breakfast. My name is Balfour. Horace Balfour. Some of you I have already met, but I cannot always put a name to your face. As you may know, for a short time I worked at Nine Fingers Charlie's Art Emporium, and I believe at least a few of you signed on with him."

"Yeah! What's going on? I heard he shot Mrs. Comstock and the place is locked up." someone shouted. "Is he in jail?"

"When do we get our work back?" another student called out.

Horace held up his hands to silence them. "I'll get to that in a minute. As you probably already know, there was a shooting, and the body of Mrs. Comstock, who some of you know as another art gallery owner, was found dead on the floor. The shop is what the police call a 'crime scene', which means it is locked. I can't do anything about that beyond asking Chief Garrison to set a time and date for you to come and claim your work. I can do that, but I can't promise that he'll go along with the idea."

"Thanks, heaps!" a woman with a sarcastic voice shouted.

Horace held up his hands again. "I know, it isn't fair and it doesn't seem right, but remember, a woman is dead. Now, if it was your mother...."

"No one liked Mrs. Comstock!" the woman retorted.

Horace smiled broadly, disarming the small crowd. "I encountered her twice and I tend to agree with you. So, let's just say, she wasn't the most warm-hearted person I've ever met. Meanwhile, let's work together. Maybe, if you can tell me more about her we'll get a clue as to why someone wanted her dead and why they wanted to kill her. That might also help us speed things along with Chief Garrison so you can get your paintings back sooner. We give him something, he gives us something."

The students remained quiet, thinking through what he was offering.

"I'm going to spend some time out here this morning. There's a nice swing out on the porch. It's got a good view of the meadow and the lagoon..."

A woman cut him off, "You can't smoke your pipe out there. Mrs. Walters doesn't allow it."

"I see. Well, since she is my daughter-in-law we'll keep some peace on the family. I'll be on the swing or I'll take a chair and sit out on the meadow and look at the lagoon." Horace continued. "I think you'll agree with that idea because I've seen a lot of your paintings are of that scene. Everyone seems to like it. Either that, or you don't want to walk too far. That goes for me, too, so, that's where I'll be. You want to talk, lend a hand, and come see me."

"You gonna keep our names out of this?" a young man asked.

"As much as possible. At my age, I don't always remember things, you know. Course, if you tell me you're the one who plugged her, then I might remember that."

The group laughed.

"So, let's get to work cracking this case. I'll be here as long as it takes, all morning if need be," Horace said

Fred looked in at the Princess Cafe and another small diner, but didn't see anyone at the tables. At Dominic's barbershop he had a little more luck. "Comstock? Yeah, I know him. He used to come in for a haircut. He wasn't much of a talker, though. Quiet as Silent Cal himself; couldn't get two words out of him. Hair cut, dust the back of his neck with a little Pinaud talcum powder, and that's it. Oh, and he was always a lousy tipper," the barber said. "A man with all that money, too."

"I think he looked sad, Mister," Tommy, the shoeshine boy said. "He sort of looked like he didn't have a friend in the world. Maybe he was an orphan growing up and never got over it."

"Now, that's helpful," Fred told the lad, and handed him a half-dollar piece. It wasn't much information, but Fred knew from past experience that almost anything might be helpful whether it was a medical diagnosis or a murder. And with a half-dollar tip, the boy might find some more information.

He drove around to the gas stations. At the first he leaned against Dr. Horace's car as the attendant filled the tank. Horace pumped him for information, but he didn't know Mr. Comstock or Nine

Fingers Charlie. At the second station, he had the oil and water checked. The young attendant didn't have anything to contribute.

Fred didn't want to return without something more than the thin observation of the shoeshine boy, and a quick check of the clock made him think there would be time to drive down along the lake past the Comstock place, go further south, and then come back on another road. Midweek or not, he drove with all the speed of an elderly Sunday afternoon motorist on a trip through the country, looking at every driveway, farm field, pasture, and house along the way.

The Comstock place was a small estate, at least compared to some. On the lakeside of the road was a big white wooden Victorian house with a wraparound porch, a carriage house that had been converted into a garage for the family cars, and a tennis court. Directly across the house on the other side of the road was a horse barn and a couple of smaller outbuildings, an identical pair of cottages and a small shed that looked like it was for a small car.

Fred took it all in, driving slowly, but not so slowly as to catch attention. He wasn't too worried. Everyone in town knew that Mrs. Comstock had been shot, so a good number of them had made the same pilgrimage past the family home. Some of the tourists, maybe curious or bored, or a combination of both, had also driven out. All of them were hoping to see something of more interest than a large summer house and immaculate estate. There was nothing to be seen.

The house on the lakeside of the road looked well kept. The grass was mowed, some landscaping, and the clapboard siding had a relatively fresh coat of paint. The house on other side of the road looked run down. It had been a week weeks since someone had cut the lawns, the buildings needed painting, and he hoped no guests had been sequestered in the smaller cottages.

The only thing that surprised Fred was that another quarter mile further down the road a flagman was standing on the side, waving Fred to stop. "Culvert collapsed up ahead. You can't get through, so the only thing is to turn around and go back the way you came. There's a driveway up ahead." Fred thanked him and drove back into town, slowing down again as he passed the Comstock place. It gave him a chance to look it over more carefully from a different perspective

An hour or so before dinner Fred, Theo and Clarice, and Horace met in his study. One by one they told what they had learned. "Thunderation! In other words, we aren't much further ahead tonight than we were this morning," Horace growled.

"That's about the size of it," Theo agreed. "What about you, big brother?"

"The students at Ox-Bow all liked Nine Fingers Charlie, but they're pretty sore about their art being locked up," Horace summed it up.

"No one knew much about Mr. Comstock, at least not in town. I couldn't even get much out of the banker except that Comstock was a railroad lawyer," Fred said.

Theo interrupted, "And we already knew that."

"And no one had much nice to say about Mrs. Comstock," added Clarice. "Maybe the only good that has come out of it is that people know you're working on the case, Horace. Oh, and she cheated at mah-jong , and then got angry if someone caught her."

He looked at her and said, "We're getting nowhere."

"That's about what the chief must be feeling, too," Theo said. "Horace, I don't think it would hurt for us to talk with him and let him know what we've found out..."

"...haven't found out!" Horace interrupted.

"...found out, haven't found out. Maybe it'll do some good. Maybe not."

"What *have* you learned that I ought to be knowing?" Chief Garrison asked, surprising everyone in the study as he stood in the ship's study doorway.

"That's just what we were talking about. We've been all over the place trying to find anything, and so far – goose eggs," Theo answered.

"Goose eggs! Why are you wasting your time looking for goose eggs when we've got a murderer to find? I told you we know who did it; we just have to find out where he is," he snarled. "I'm beginning to think I ought to run you in and charge you with being an accessory after the fact!"

No one noticed Phoebe walking past the open door. She moved quickly, then leaned against the wall, catching her breath.

She stood out of sight near the door, hoping to hear more.

NINE

Phoebe was unusually quiet all during dinner. "I don't think she's getting enough rest," Harriet said when Clarice noticed her silence. "Maybe she's trying to do too much before school starts."

"I am sufficiently well rested, Mother," Phoebe said with a protracted sigh of disgust. She was becoming increasingly irritated and prickly with being discussed in the third person as if she was not even present at the table. It was a terrible fault of grown-ups, and she was determined never to do it once she got older. Even more, she wanted her mother and the rest of her family to stop now.

She was not tired, but worried. Very worried, about all that was happening to her grandfather. She knew something was very wrong, but had not put together all the pieces.

"What does 'accessory after the fact' mean?" she asked Harriet on their walk home.

"Where ever did you hear such a thing?" she asked.

"I overheard Chief Garrison say he might arrest Grandfather as an accessory after the fact. So what does that mean?"

Harriet stopped walking and turned toward her daughter, her eyes narrowed in anger. "You mean, you were eaves dropping when you heard Chief Garrison, don't you?"

"Well, yes. But, not really. I was walking past the door to the study and it was open and the police chief was shouting, so it wasn't like I was really trying to snoop on purpose or anything. I just sort of had my ears open when the door was open," Phoebe tried to explain, perhaps a bit too quickly.

"I see. Well, it means you got yourself all worked up listening to adults having conversations that you weren't intended to hear. It isn't polite, and it certainly isn't being on your best Paris Manners, now is it?" Harriet asked.

"No, I guess not," she admitted, softly. When they arrived at home Phoebe said she was tired and was going to bed.

Harriet quietly slipped into her daughter's bedroom and sat on the edge of the bed, softly stroking the girl's hair. "Are you awake?" she whispered.

"Yes, but I'm trying to pretend I'm asleep so you won't stop," Phoebe answered.

"Dear, I'm sorry about being short with you on the walk home. I know you're worried about your grandfather. Well, the truth is, so am I. I'm not certain about this, but I think the police chief might have meant that your grandfather knows more than he is telling him. It wouldn't surprise me if he does, but I really think the chief is bluffing, so there's no need to worry. You can sleep tight tonight, all right?"

"All right. And Mother, you sleep tight and don't let the bed bugs bite, too." Phoebe smiled as her mother kissed her on the forehead and tucked her in.

"I remember just a few years ago when you always wanted a story about the fairies who lived outside your bedroom window," Harriet thought to herself. Now her daughter had a part time job and was worried about others. She was growing up and it was discomforting. It was happening far too fast.

It was about the same time that Phoebe was drifting off to sleep in her bed that Horace asked Fred, "Are you up for a little walk?"

"Yeah, and I get the idea that you want to do a little scouting around," he answered.

Horace nodded. "You know who we haven't seen around here the past couple of days?" Before Fred could say anything his boss answered his own question. "Those two gold digger twins haven't been around."

"Say, you done did come up with a good one. I'd sort of forgotten about those two. I guess I just figured they'd come up on a steamer for a day or two and gone back where they came from. Let's shake a leg and see what we can see!" Fred said with enthusiasm.

"Let's wander around town a bit, and then make our way over to the Big Pavilion. Any idea what's happening there tonight?" Horace asked.

"The ad in the Commercial Record said the *Clevelanders and Ted Stacks.* You ever hear of them?"

Horace gave him a withering look. "Thunderation, no! Has anyone? I thought it was someone called Miff Mole. They don't stay long, do they? Now, keep your eyes peeled for those two dolly-twins."

They wandered past Parrish's soda fountain, looked in, then moved on without much luck. None of the cafes or restaurants yielded any better results, and finally Horace nodded toward the front door of the dance hall. "Fred, you circle around to the left side; I'll take the right, and we'll meet back up here. And listen, if you run into someone you know, see if they've seen the two women."

"You want that maybe I should tell them you're looking for a couple of girls?" Fred teased.

"Thunderation!" Horace explained in disgust. "Just get to work. We need a break."

"What we need is that there Doc Howell back down here. She's the brains of this outfit," he muttered once he was out of earshot of his employer. The two men slowly made their way down the sides of the main hall, carefully looking over the patrons. It was all flappers and men with slicked back hair. Here and there were older men and society matrons. Horace and Fred passed each other near the front, then continued their way around to the back where they met up again.

They agreed to stay for another hour or so, taking a table at the back, nearest the door. "They come in and we'll spot 'em, and that there is for sure!" Fred said optimistically. Horace was not quite so certain.

"Listen, Fred, a couple of times when we were here you walked over to see some men you knew who were sitting at that table over on the left side. Is that them?"

"Some of them, sure looks like it. It's a little hard to tell from this far away."

"Then why don't you go speak to them and sound them out?" Horace asked.

"Sure thing, Doc. And I know – be real discreet about it. Don't give away our plans to the enemy. Say, maybe if I get the chance, I can find out if they know anything about Nine Fingers Charlie, too."

Horace nodded in agreement. He watched as Fred worked his way across the room and joined five or six men at a table. It was nearly half an hour before he returned.

"Skunked. I got pretty razzed asking about the two blondes, but I eventually got it out of them that no one's seen them. Course, they want me to introduce them if we do find them," Fred reported. That sort is always looking for a good time girl."

"And Nine Fingers Charlie? Anything?"

"I'm not certain. The name rung a bell with a couple of them, and one of the old-timers sort of whistles a bit and said something about that being a name out of the past.," Fred told him.

"I've had enough of this racket." He nodded toward the band on the stage. "Listen, if you hear of someone taking up a free-will offering to buy music lessons for that fellow, put me down for a ten spot. Thunderation!" Horace exploded. "Time to call it a night and have some peace and quiet." He pointed toward the exit door, then hurriedly led Fred outside.

"What else did you learn?" Horace asked once they were outside.

"Well, it's like this. I mentioned the name Nine Finger Charlie, and one of those old boys sort of came to life all of a sudden. I mean, he looked up, and then tried to hide it by looking down again. Dead give-aways, if you were to ask me, so I knew he had heard of him before."

"Now that is interesting. If those boys have heard of Nine Finger Charlie, then it looks like my former boss had a more interesting past than studying economics. Fred, by any chance do you know if those fellows are in town a while longer?" Horace asked.

"I done did think about that, so when I was leaving I said 'I'll see you tomorrow, maybe,' and they didn't say anything about leaving town right away. My hunch is they're probably here for a while."

"That is good news. We just might be making some progress," Horace said. He relit his pipe. "Good news, Sergeant. Good news."

"I wouldn't be telling you what to do, but I sure hope you're not getting ahead of yourself," Fred said cautiously.

Sleep did not come easily to any of them that night. Harriet and Phoebe were both awake in their beds, staring up at the ceiling, thinking about the way the police chief had been so threatening to Horace. Theo was worried about his brother, if for no other reason that he was his brother. And Fred was tossing and turning, twice troubled during the night by memories of the Great War. As he had done for years, when Horace returned to his cabin he lifted the picture of his late wife out of the top drawer, taking one final look before turning off the lights.

TEN

Harriet was awake much earlier than usual, and when Phoebe was up about an hour later, she found her mother at the kitchen table finishing up a letter. Harriet held up a finger to stop Phoebe from interrupting, then finished, and folded it up as she said, "Good morning." The two talked for a few minutes before Harriet announced she had to go to Ox-Bow for an early meeting. "There is still some coffee left, if you would like some. Maybe two cups," Harriet told her. It seemed so ordinary that Phoebe didn't suspect a thing.

Harriet needed to get Beatrix's address from the register in the Ox-Bow office. She found it and wrote it on the front of the envelop and then drove to the Post Office in Douglas to mail it. "I'd like this to get there as quickly as possible," she told the postmaster. "Perhaps airmail special delivery?"

"That'll cost you a lot more, you know, Mrs. Walters," he said. "Regular mail is three cents. It's a lot more sending it airmail and special delivery. You sure it's that important?"

"It is."

Harriet wasn't the only correspondent early that morning. Clarice was in the library, writing a letter that she also wanted to go out that morning. And, as Phoebe was having her coffee to wake up, she thought about her mother's letter writing and that led her to realize she had a letter that she needed to write.

"You know, it occurred to me that you'd mentioned something about Nine Fingers Charlie teaching at that Episcopal boys' school in Minnesota," Theo said to Horace over their morning coffee.

"Yes, what of it?"

"Now, don't you think it might be a good idea to send a wire up there and see if they have any records that might tell us more about him? It might give us an idea as to where he's gone to lay low for a while," Theo suggested.

"Good point. And, while we're at it, maybe we can find this Professor Stephen Leacock as well and ask him," Horace answered. "Seems to me that Nine Fingers Charlie mentioned McGill University up in Canada." At first Theo didn't know whether or not his brother was being sarcastic. "Can't hurt to gather a little more information," Horace added.

Theo finished his coffee, stood up, and said, "Well then, Western Union ought to be open by now. I'll get on with it."

Horace said nothing. He pulled out his pipe, filled and lit it, and stared out across the river to the other side, lost in thought. He didn't see Fred spot Phoebe as she was about to come up the gangplank. He raced down the boards to intercept and talk with her before she saw her grandfather. They whispered to each other, then nodded in agreement about something.

Horace hadn't noticed them, but Doctor Landis did as he was driving down Water Street. He pulled over and jumped out. "Doctor Horace in, by any chance?" he asked. Fred told him he was sitting on the deck.

"Horace, I came to apologize and ask you to forgive me," Landis said, his right hand extended.

"Apologize for what?" he asked, pretending to be surprised.

"I blundered and you got the blunt end of the stick. Look, I was wrong when I asked if you would take a few days off from working for me. I'd heard some of the prattling old-timers saying that you were mixed up in that murder, and thought .... Well, the truth is, I didn't think. I reacted. I put my fears, or something, ahead of friendship, and I was wrong."

"Ah, don't think anything of it. I've been keeping a bit busy lately as it is," Horace said.

"The thing is, I know I'm a good doctor, but I'm not certain I'm a good small town doctor. It's all a lot different from growing up in Pittsburgh...." his voice trailed off.

"I know. Theo and I grew up in a small town, but then when we became physicians there were older people who still thought of us as a couple of cut-ups. Pretty much the same, in a way, as what you've got here. I can see why that position at the sanatorium was so appealing," Horace said slowly.

"Not was – is. It is still appealing. In fact...."

Horace interrupted, "In fact, you were planning on taking your family up north to look over the facility and town."

Doctor Landis smiled. "Yeah, that's about the gist of it. I think you saw right through me, didn't you?"

"You'll never know until you look it over, that's for sure. And I commend you for taking along your wife and boys. They need to see it."

"So, perhaps you could fill in...?" he asked tentatively.

Horace smiled. "Always happy to help. Tomorrow?"

"How about this afternoon, if you don't mind. I'll show you where I keep everything and you won't have to go searching," Landis smiled, standing up to leave.

"See you at noon. Say, if something comes up on my end, Theo will be available to substitute, if that's all right with you," Horace suggested. "Looks like Chief Garrison expects us to pull his irons out of the fire – again."

"Better than all right!"

Noon brought better news than Fred and Phoebe dared expect. Horace would be at the hospital, and Mr. Higgins at Western Union would be out for his hour-long lunch. He always came back an hour later, his breath smelling unusually sweet, and ask if everything was okay. He never waited for an answer, but went straight into his office and closed the door.

"Phoebs, you need me to write this out for you?" Fred asked as he came in the door. "I just saw Higgins going down the street, so I figured the coast is clear. You sure he never comes back early?"

She smiled. "Just take your time speaking. I'll send it straight out."

"And you have Doctor Howell's address, don't you?" he asked.

"Right here. Hold on a moment." She quickly tapped out the name and address. "Ready when you are!"

"Doc Howell. Boss is over his head with a murder. Mrs. Comstock victim; 9 Fingers Charlie suspect. No clues. Chief threatens H as accessory after fact. Please advice. Fred Epsilon."

"Epsilon?" Phoebe asked. "I didn't know that was your last name."

"It isn't," Fred said. "It's sort of a password between Doc Howell and me. She'll know its extra-special important. We'll hear from her in no time."

"Do you think she'll come back to Saugatuck?" Phoebe asked.

"Ah, she don't need to do that. Why, she can sit in her rocking chair back in Minnesota, light up a big old stogey, and in no time have it all figured out and that'll be it. 'Sides, she just went home, so she won't want to be coming back."

"Just like that? You sure?" Phoebe asked.

"Well, something like that, anyways. You just keep your eyes peeled for a message back here. Say, she won't know where to send a wire back, will she? Better send her a second one. Tell her the first one was from me and to answer through you here in the afternoons."

Phoebe tapped out the second message. "Do you think Grandfather will be angry we did this?" she asked.

"Might be, but we're just trying to help out a little. Anyway, it's water under the bridge now. The deed is done." Fred said as he looked down at the telegraph key. "Guess we'll have to wait and see." He looked at his watch and whistled. "Time for me to act like a caisson and get rolling along. Take care." With that, he was out the door.

"Where's Doctor Balfour?" the police chief demanded when he came aboard the *Aurora* and saw Doctor Theo in the library.

"Right here. I'm Doctor Balfour," Theo answered with a sly smile.

"You know very well which one of you two I want. Where is he?"

"Probably at the hospital with Doctor Landis. Something I could do for you?" Theo asked.

"Well, maybe you could, long as I'm here I've got some questions for you. Maybe you know something about this Nine Fingers Charlie fellow, or maybe your brother told you something I ought to be knowing. So, just *what* do you know?" the chief asked firmly, pulling up a chair.

"Not a thing. Probably less than Horace because I just met the man once in passing. And Horace hasn't told me anything other than that he was an interesting conversationalist and obviously well read."

"And that's it?" the chief asked.

"And that's it," Theo answered. "Now, I have a question for you. What have you been able to learn from Mr. Comstock that might help Horace to solve the murder for you?"

The chief said nothing for a quarter of a minute, then his jaw dropped and his eyebrows knit together in anger. "That's police business! That's for me to know, and not a couple of amateurs who ought to be minding their manners! Besides, it isn't proper etiquette to start taking a statement from a fellow when his wife just bought the farm!" He stood up and marched off.

ELEVEN

"Thunderation! A full week of work since Mrs. Comstock was killed, and all we've got to show for it is a pair of telegrams, and nothing helpful from either of them!" Horace rapped his knuckles against his study desk.

"Well, a little more than that. The dean at the Episcopal school and Stephen Leacock both wrote they haven't heard of Nine Fingers Charlie, so it is beginning to look more and more like he was telling some big lies to cover something up," Theo said firmly.

Horace was quiet for a minute, then said softly. "Yes, you're right. And Garrison hasn't had any luck finding him, so at least we're one up on him."

"I didn't know it was a contest," Theo replied. "Looks like Nine Fingers Charlie is long gone. This just might be an unsolved murder for a long time. Maybe it'll never be closed."

"The way things are going, it isn't ever going to get solved," Horace said "at least not in our lifetime." He was silent for a full minute as he took out his pipe, filled and then lit it. "Anyway, it isn't exactly our line of work, is it? I just want it resolved so my name isn't dragged into it." Suddenly he changed the subject. "Say, have you walked up Hoffman Street? Someone is building a nice looking house up there."

"Well, now that is exciting," Theo said sarcastically. "What brought that up?"

"Here's the thing. It's more like they're putting it together. Everything came in a boxcar and then got hauled up there by truck. All they have to do now is follow the instructions and put it together. It's fascinating!" Horace said. "You should see it."

"And just *why* is that so interesting?" Theo asked.

"Well, I was at the site earlier today, and the foreman said that they can add a carriage house, an apartment in the back, almost anything the owner wants."

"I won't even ask why you find it so interesting," Theo yawned.

"Well, I've been thinking that maybe we can apply it to medicine," Horace said.

"Apply it to medicine? Horace, that's a daft idea if I ever heard one!"

"Might be, but until you think it through you'll never know. Say, I'm going to walk up there before I go over to the hospital. You want to come along?" Horace offered.

Theo looked at his watch. "Clarice has got me sitting on ice for at least another half hour. Sure. Up and then straight back , for me at least. You can look at this magical house to your heart's content."

When they arrived at the job site Theo was still not impressed. "Well, it's interesting, but I don't understand your fascination with it."

"It's the fact that every stick of wood, all the electrical wiring, everything, is all manufactured at one site, moved here, and then assembled. It's fast, simple, and straight forward," Horace answered as he watched the carpenters at work.

"And what happens if the people next door decide to buy the identical house? Next thing you know, you'll have a whole city full of identical houses. Who'd want that?" Theo challenged. Horace was focused on watching the progress on the house and didn't hear the question, or answer it. In frustration, Theo said it was time for him to return to the boat and meet Clarice. "I still don't see how this has anything to do with medicine," Theo said as he departed. Horace was fascinated with the construction project and mumbled something about seeing him later in the afternoon when he came back from the hospital.

Much to Theo's surprise, he found Clarice and Harriet sitting close together, talking with each other about something that was obviously important. "I think you should be in on this, Theo," Harriet told him.

She waited for him to sit down and after a moment regained her courage. "You and Horace might not approve of this, but I wrote to Beatrix and told her about the murder. I did it because, well, you know that Chief Garrison can be like, and I hoped to bring this to an end before he arrested Horace. All I did was ask for some ideas or suggestions."

"That seems like a reasonable thing," Theo said. "Is there any news from her?

"Yes, a telegram this morning," Harriet said quietly. "Beatrix promised to investigate and apparently she did. She's still gathering information before she sends it to us."

"And, how could this not be anything other than good news?" Theo asked.

"You know what your brother is like. After Beatrix took off so fast a couple of weeks ago, well, I assumed they had a big falling out, and that he wouldn't like it if I wrote to Beatrix because he might be thinking I'm meddling by trying to get them back together or something like that, which I absolutely am not trying to do, if that makes any sense, because I thought we really needed her perspective."

Clarice reached and put her hand on Harriet's hands. "Of course it does. But dear, next time catch your breath in the middle of a long sentence."

"I'm sorry," she answered.

"Don't be," Theo told her. "You know what those two are like. Beatrix left because her summer holiday was over, that's all."

"And Horace didn't say anything to her?"

"No."

"And she didn't say anything that set him off?"

"No. It's simple, Harriet. Beatrix came for the summer like always, and she went home like always. 'Lord willing and the creek don't rise,' as William S. Hart would say, she'll be back here next summer; same as always."

"Well, that's a relief," Harriet smiled thinly. "And, maybe she'll find something out that will be helpful."

"I think you did the right thing contacting Beatrix. If she can find something useful, then it is a very good thing you've done for all of us," Clarice said.

"That is such a relief," Harriet repeated.

"There's something more you should know, Theo," Clarice told her husband.

"What?"

"I think you should know that Mrs. Comstock was not very well liked by many of the women in Saugatuck. Well, at least not by her circle of friends."

"That doesn't make sense. How could she have friends who didn't like her?" Theo asked.

"Well, her circle of friends were mainly the women who are active in the social, the cultural life, of the community. They belong to committees that hold the art fairs and organize events to raise money for worthy causes..." Clarice began.

"Only they end up squabbling. That part I understand," her husband interrupted.

"Yes. Only it is more than squabbles. They all want to be in charge and then get others to do the real work. And they all try to out-do the others. It's more than squabbles and disagreements; it's bitter rivalry and long-held grudges. Before long they drag their children and husbands into it."

"Then why do they bother with these projects in the first place?" Theo asked.

"Because, once the event is over they all make nice with each other again," Clarice said with a big sigh of disappointment that Theo did not understand.

"I'm not certain I follow your drift, but how does it tie in with the fact Mrs. Comstock was shot?"

"All I'm saying is that while you and Horace are thinking it had to have been Nine Fingers Charlie, the real killer might be someone else."

"I'll be you have several names you could give me," Theo suggested.

"Yes. You might want to have a long talk with Miss Symington for starters. And after her, I'd talk to Mrs. Vandenberg. The two of them and Mrs. Comstock all despised each other. I'd start with those two. You might get an earful of news," Clarice said.

"But wait a minute," Harriet said. "Mrs. Comstock was found inside Nine Finger Charlie's gallery and the door was locked. So, how did someone get the key, lure her there, shoot and kill her, lock the door, and then get away?"

"That *would* be a challenge, but never put it past an angry woman to get revenge," Clarice said.

"Say, I've got a question for you," Theo said to Harriet, eager to change the subject. "My brother has got a new bee in his bowler hat. He is absolutely fixated on that house being up the hill; the one made by Sears and Roebuck, and comes ready to be built."

"I know the one you mean, and there are a couple of more. But not everyone likes them, and there were a few people who tried to convince the village council to outlaw them," Harriet answered.

"That's nutty," Theo answered. "Why?"

"Oh, they didn't like the way they look, and some said that it was taking jobs away from men who need the work. Just things like that. Anyway, I need to get some work done today. Theo, if you and Clarice want to know more about the houses, you might have Fred take you to the Sears store in Holland. But if you want to know more to figure out Horace, well, good luck!" She laughed.

TWELVE

Captain Garwood was in the pilothouse of the *Aurora* and the first to hear the sound of an engine far off in the distance. From the start he didn't think it was a boat. The sound was wrong for a larger cabin cruiser, and it seemed to be moving too fast even for speedboat. He searched the river with his binoculars, then noticed a tiny speck, still out over the lake, low over the water. It disappeared for a while behind the dunes and then came up the Kalamazoo River. "I don't believe it," he said to himself. It was a yellow bi-plane, and he would have made a sizeable wager that he knew the owner.

"Fred! Incoming!" he shouted down to the deck below, pointing up to the sky. Fred cupped his hands over his eyes to block the sun as he strained to get a better look.

"You think...?" he shouted to the captain.

"No doubt about it! Better go out to the airfield and haul her in."

"Yessirree, Bob, I'd better do just that, toot and sweet, and right away!"

They watched as the plane flew just over the water, pulling up as she whisked over the boat, climbed further, and circled to make its way to the field.

"Is that who I think it is?" Mrs. Garwood called out from the galley, looking at the plane.

"It sure is!" Fred answered. "Doc Beatrix Howell, herself! Better put another plate out for dinner! It's the air corps to the rescue!"

Mrs. Garwood stared at him, not yet willing to share in his joy and excitement.

Horace had not heard the plane because he was in the hospital operating room setting the arm of a young boy who had tried becoming a glider pilot from the top of his father's carriage house, using his mother's tablecloth as a parachute. It had not been a successful flight.

"That hurts!" the boy objected as Horace and Nurse VanderBos began putting the splint into place and bandaging it before applying the plaster cast.

"Of course it does," Horace said. "You're lucky it was just your arm you broke and not your head. Now, settle down fly-boy, so we can get you bandaged up, and then we'd better look at those scraped up knees."

"And you should remember that if God wanted you to fly, He would have given you wings!" the nurse added firmly.

" I don't think he needs to worry about that. His mother is going to have him grounded for a good long time," Horace answered.

As he was scrubbing the last of the plaster off his hands, Horace talked with the boy's mother. "Just keep him settled down for the day. By tomorrow he'll be just fine, and let him have his bragging rights about being a tough patient. That will keep his mind off the break. Just keep him off the roof; both feet solidly on the ground. And you might have a word with the other mothers to warn them against their boys trying the same sort of thing."

"Thank you, Doctor. I know it's a bit of an imposition, but I didn't want to leave Maud and Jeff at home on their own, worried about their brother, so I brought them with me. I was wondering, as long as we're here....well, you know, with school starting soon, and all," she asked.

"Of course," he said. "Jeff first, and then bring Maud in." Horace smiled as he remembered the warning Dr. Landis had given him about last minute and unexpected "add-ons." Almost instantly he was lost in his own thoughts. Years ago he and Theo and their first partner had their own steady stream of add-ons, usually farm families who had come to town for their Friday night shopping. The three doctors made a point of never charging for each patient – just one family member. If they had the money, that is.

But that had changed over the decades. The practice had grown and the physicians no longer collected their own fees and turned the cash over to their bookkeeper. Their first book keeper, Jack Hempe, had been replaced by a trained accountant who, in turn, was replaced by an office full of financial people. Horace chafed against it, claiming that it depersonalized medical care.

It meant that if the mother had brought in her son for a broken arm and then wanted two more children examined, some secretary would have been writing it down. By the time Dr. Horace was finished, the bill would have been drawn up and ready to be presented.

He breathed deeply and smiled: Thankfully, Landis still maintained the old traditions that care for the patient comes first.

It was the faint whiff of cigar smoke that caught Horace's attention as he stepped onto his boat late that afternoon. To his surprise, the aroma energized him and he picked up his pace as he walked to his study and opened the door.

"Hello, Horace!" a very familiar voice said to him. Beatrix swivelled the chair behind his desk around to face him. "Busy day at the office?"

"You're here!" he said stunned.

"Sherlock, what a magnificent statement of the obvious. Yes. I have been reading a lot about you lately, and thought I had better come join the party."

"What do you mean?" he asked, sitting down in the big leather chair opposite her.

"Well, several telegrams and letters about the mysterious Nine Fingers Charlie Larsen. And something about the chief wanting to take you in for questioning. Accessory after the fact? Horace, that's a new one, even for you."

"What are you talking about?" he asked. "All that get into the Minnesota papers?"

"No. It seems your family is very concerned. Phoebe, Harriet, Clarice, even Fred. By the way, thank you for holding on to the cigars. I found them in the top left drawer of your desk. Something to drink? I will be 'mother' and pour," she offered. Horace nodded.

"This is very uncomfortable," Beatrix said as she stood up. "You are in my chair. Do you mind?" It wasn't a question, and she motioned to his own chair behind the desk. They exchanged positions and she asked, "Better?"

"Much," Horace answered.

"Yes, for me, as well," she said. "That was very odd. Let us resolve not to make that mistake again."

"Perhaps it would be helpful to start from the beginning," Beatrix suggested.

For the next few minutes Horace told her how he had met Nine Fingers Charlie right after she left Saugatuck to return home, and was offered a job.

"That is unusual," she said softly. "You walk in off the street as a complete stranger, you know little or nothing about art or an art gallery, and after a few minutes he hires you. Did that not seem odd to you? It brings to mind Conan Doyle's 'The Red-Headed League,' and perhaps for some nefarious reasons of his own."

"In a way, yes. But frankly, I found it rather amusing. I assumed he had no idea what I did for a living and thought I was some fairly decently dressed old codger who could use some extra money. He seemed to take a rather casual attitude toward the business," Horace said, his unease beginning to grow.

"And this Mrs. Comstock? What was she like?" Harriet asked.

For the next ten minutes Horace told Beatrix the same thing he had told Chief Garrison and his family. He explained about Mrs. Comstock's sudden appearance in the store, her silent husband waiting behind her, and then her demands and threats before she stormed out the door. "You can perhaps find out more about her from Harriet. They have a long history through Ox- Bow," Horace added.

"Is that Lorenzo Comstock the attorney for the CB&Q Railroad?" Beatrix asked.

"Yes. No. Well, maybe. I know he was a railroad lawyer," Horace said, flustered. "I don't recall hearing his first name."

Beatrix looked at Horace and said flatly, "I think it is best if the others were present so we all hear everything at the same time. It is almost time for dinner, so we will wait." Not surprisingly, Horace groaned in frustration and concluded with a raspy "Thunderation!"

Fred carried two extra chairs as they all crowded into Horace's study. "Thank you for letting me know about this little mystery," Beatrix said with a slight smile. "I hate being left out of murder, mayhem, and intrigue. And this one is fascinating.

"Horace told me about the murder of Mrs. Comstock and about Nine Fingers Charlie. And, I am aware that Chief Garrison and you have not been able to make much progress. That explains why the chief would love to arrest Horace for being an accessory after the fact. It is his frustration and he is taking it out on others – once again, I might add, as well as to make himself look good.

"There is a very good reason why you have had little success. Mr. Charles Larsen, Nine Fingers Charlie, as you call him, is not his real name!" Beatrix paused to let the news sink in.

"Then if he isn't Nine Fingers Charlie, who is he?" Fred asked.

Beatrix smiled. "That is the story."

"Is that why we got telegrams from the dean at the boy's school in Faribault and Stephen Leacock that they didn't know him?" Theo asked.

Almost immediately Clarice chimed in, asking, "Beatrix, who is he? Don't keep us in suspense, please."

She held up her hands to regain control. "All right. To 'cut to the chase scene' as they say in the moving pictures, your Nine Fingers Charlie Larson is Clarence Lessington who before that was Clive Lossman, who before that was Clyde Lovington. He may have had other aliases before that. He is what is best known as a conman, or a con artist. Obviously, he found it necessary to move from place to place rather quickly and each time would change his name. His first mistake is that he continued using the same initials. Regrettably, many con artists make this mistake, if only because it is easier to remember their new identity." Beatrix looked at the Balfours and Fred staring back at her in shock.

"It's interesting that he should have mentioned Stephen Leacock. Leacock studied in Montreal, and Nine Fingers was indeed there, working as a teller at the Zarossi Bank, which had primarily an Italian clientele. The name of the bank and its clientele are not important. What is important is that it was also where Charles Ponzi perfected his scheme...," Beatrix continued.

"Ponzi? *The* Ponzi of the Ponzi Scheme?" Horace asked. "Thunderation!"

"The one and the same. I suspect they parted company when Mr. Ponzi was fired and the bank failed. Nonetheless, our Nine Fingers Charlie had developed a taste for what might be called the good life, and he used his charm and duplicity on both sides of the boarder. We should also note that his original connection with Mr. Ponzi, who was of Italian origins, opened some doors to several of the gangs in eastern Canada and New York, which led to him being encouraged by Arnold Rothstein's gang to take up the habit of breaking into safes.

"Nine Fingers Charlie was, perhaps still is, one of those rare individuals who does not have fingerprints, and this led him into a very successful career as a burglar and safe-cracker. In short, no evidence, no way of tracing him," Beatrix said.

"I am impressed," Theo said quietly. "That explains why Rothstein would be interested in him."

"You will perhaps be all the more impressed when I tell you that he is a very accomplished actor. Once he selects a target he studies not only the surroundings, but the people, so that he could easily blend in without suspicion. He has played the role of a mailman and a milkman, a physician, even a former member of Congress."

"Well, there you have it! Biggest bunch of crooks around!" Fred burst out.

"A physician would work well. It's the perfect reason to have a stethoscope and carry a bag for the swag," Clarice giggled.

"Very funny, dear," Theo told her.

"You will be relieved to know that he was apprehended on several occasions, the last time in St Paul, Minnesota where he had travelled to empty the contents of a Mr. Hill's safe," Beatrix said.

"How?" Horace asked. "How did he get caught?"

"Well, he had the safe door open and was helping himself to a considerable amount of cash when something or someone entered the room. Nine Fingers hid around to the side of the safe, and very foolishly kept his left fifth finger in the door as a prop. Someone slammed it shut, cutting off his finger."

"But if he didn't have fingerprints, how did they know it was him?" Theo asked.

"Charlie had the misfortune of seeking medical attention from a physician who was the brother-in-law of a police lieutenant!" Beatrix was almost cheerful. "The physician heard about the burglary and the finger inside the locked safe, and that was the end of it."

"And what became of him?" Horace asked.

"He was sentenced to ten years at the Stillwater State Prison ..." Beatrix started to explain.

Theo interrupted, "And Stillwater isn't that far from Faribault, so he re-invented himself again."

"To continue," Beatrix said firmly, "The interesting thing is that Charlie used his time wisely and became a model prisoner. He apparently spent considerable time in the prison library, primarily reading the works of John Ruskin on art."

"Thunderation! The man was constantly prattling on about Ruskin and the importance of buying new art! Well, that explains that, doesn't it?"

"Ruskin's ideas are not popular with gallery owners, and still creates considerable animosity. If Nine Fingers was putting them into effect here, it is not surprising that a high-powered gallery owner such as Mrs. Comstock would respond in vengeance," Beatrix concluded.

"Well, we know more, but I don't know that it's getting us anywhere," Theo said.

They sat in silence for several minutes, thinking over what Beatrix had told them, and trying to find the right connection to the murder. Finally Theo said, "Beatrix, you might want to hear what Clarice told Harriet and me this afternoon. It's an entirely different angle." He looked at his wife and nodded his encouragement.

THIRTEEN

"Well, now what?" Horace asked as he shook out the match he had just applied to his pipe.

"I do not have a ready-made answer, Horace," Beatrix said. "All things considered, from his past history we can safely assumed that Nine Fingers Charlie may have changed his appearance. You said he had a van Dyke beard, grey hair, and wore a grey three piece double-breasted suit. Perhaps he shaved the beard, changed his hair colour, and is wearing different clothes. Horace, he could be walking right past this boat and we wouldn't know it. However, I am quite certain that by now he is far away from here."

Horace offered his pipe to her, then said sadly, "I see what you mean. No fingerprints and an ability to change appearances. I don't suppose he has another pattern, you know, like how he always uses the same initials for his name?" Horace asked.

"Perhaps. He seems quite adept at imitating professional or businessmen," she said, returning the pipe to him.

"Let's hope not as a bank president or a branch manager," Horace chuckled.

"Or a teacher," Beatrix countered.

"Or a clergyman. This could go on forever, you know," Horace laughed. "It won't get us anywhere."

"No. Now Horace, has Chief Garrison let anyone into the gallery yet?"

"No. Not yet. At least not that I know of. Knowing him, I doubt he did much more than look at the body on the floor, glanced around for any other evidence too big to miss, and locked it up again," Horace said. "Want to at least look in the window?" He stood up and motioned toward the study door.

"There is not much to be learned from here," Beatrix said. "Have you talked with him about getting inside?"

"I did. I told him the students wanted their art back, but he was firm – the place is a crime scene and it is under lock and key until he changes his mind. And, I'm not exactly his favorite person right now."

"Horace, you have never been his favorite person," Beatrix said flatly.

"Thank you for reminding me," he answered.

She stared through the large windows at the paintings hanging on the wall. "They must get them returned; the students deserve it," she said quietly.

"You could talk with him in the morning, perhaps suggest that if he gives permission to the students he could be there when they come to collect their work. That would give him a chance to watch them for anything suspicious and talk to them one at a time," Horace suggested.

"That might work, Horace," she answered. "And you can keep him occupied while I see if there are any clues."

"You mean 'snoop', don't you?"

"Horace, I am a lady, and a lady does not snoop. I will simply be looking for any clues and evidence. Perhaps the important point to make with the chief is that it will afford him an opportunity to talk with the artists who had contact with Nine Fingers."

They moved on from the gallery and strolled around Saugatuck, going down one side of Butler Street and up the other. Crossing the street ahead of them, on their way to the Big Pavilion, was a couple of young women. "Those two remind me of something I haven't told you. There is something else, although I can't see how it could be connected with Nine Fingers Charlie. A couple of blonde flappers came into the gallery one day and got rather flirty with him."

"With just him? Two on one? That is odd. Two on two, perhaps?"

"A bit," Horace admitted, his face reddening.

Beatrix ignored his discomfort. "Most likely they were little more than a couple of high-spirited young women who found pleasure in teasing, and were in hopes that Nine Fingers Charlie would pay for a night out on the town. Knowing what we do about Saugatuck, they probably came up on a steamer for a night or two and have now returned.

More importantly, is there anything else you remember?"

"Only that Nine Fingers called her 'Curdleface' once she left the gallery," he answered. Beatrix stopped to look at him, bewildered at his answer. "No, not the two flappers. He referred to Mrs. Comstock as 'Curdleface.'"

"That is an interesting nickname, but I do not believe it is relevant," Beatrix said, as they continued walking toward the police station.

To their surprise the chief agreed to their idea of returning the artwork to the students. "Doctor Howell, you're right about that giving me a chance to talk with everyone of those students about our killer. No telling what I'll learn!"

"Yes, and perhaps they will be less wary in the gallery since they will be focused on the return of their work," she added. "Until tomorrow at nine, then. Doctor Balfour and I will go to Ox-Bow to inform the students."

Later that evening, when they had returned from the school, Beatrix asked Horace to sketch out the floor plan of the shop so they could be prepared for the morning. "This way we can keep, or at least try to keep, Chief Garrison facing away from the back of the shop and the back room. Horace, if he objects, point out that from where he will be sitting he can keep an eye on the artists and talk to them while you help them get the paintings and check them off the list. If you can keep him focused, all the better. If he loses his focus, a loud 'thunderation!' will be my signal to watch out."

It was getting late and they were both stifling a series industrial-strength yawns. "By the way, Beatrix, thank you for the Wodehouse book. It's a delight," Horace said.

"Welcome. But tonight I have something else for you to read. The reason I came down here was to deliver the newspapers. Well, at least the clippings. 'Special, Special, Read all about it. Nine Fingers Charlie on trial,'" she said. She opened a valise and handed him a stack of newspapers. "Some bedtime reading for you."

"Where did you get these?" Horace asked.

"I know someone who works in the morgue for the news service used by the Twin City papers. They're on loan, so don't lose any. And if something should break on Nine Fingers Charlie, I have to get them back to her immediately," Beatrix explained.

Horace was up earlier than usual and had gone through several cups of coffee before anyone was on deck. When Beatrix joined him she asked, "Well?"

"Well?" Well what?"

"Yes. What did you learn?"

"Plenty," he said. "I learned that this fellow Bertie Wooster and his friends drink far too much, and that he is terrified of his valet." He paused and winked. "If you mean what did I learn from the newspapers, the answer is the same – plenty."

"I thought you might. Really, Horace, you should broaden your reading. Do you not think that reading about Nine Finger Charlie is far more interesting than a new way to suture of gall bladder?"

"All things considered, yes," he smiled. "And, after reading all of that, I don't feel so bad about being taken in by him. He's a true expert."

Their plan worked better than they anticipated. They arrived a few minutes early and moved a desk and chair for the chief so he faced the door and could interview one artist at a time. He agreed with Horace that by sitting there he could better watch all of the artists and the street. While he kept busy with the questions and taking their statements, Horace collected their artwork and handed it over. Meanwhile, Beatrix carefully worked her way from the rear of the gallery into the backroom. From there, she silently padded up the stairs into the two rooms on the second floor. Two and a half hours later, the last student was done and the gallery was empty of paintings.

"All right, you two, time to get out. I'm locking the place up and it's going to stay that way," the chief ordered. Horace had to contain himself not to appear too eager to leave the store and the chief so he could talk with Beatrix. They stood and watched as the chief locked the door.

"Of course, sooner or later the owner will want to get in there and find a new tenant," Horace reminded the chief. He received a snort of disgust.

"Absolutely nothing. Nothing, Horace. Not a single scrap of incriminating paper. There were some art magazines, but nothing secreted between the pages. It is almost pristine."

"That's not helpful," Horace moaned. "From what I read in the newspaper articles, he was an absolute professional, so maybe he was careful not to leave anything incriminating."

"No, Horace. It was more than that, and it is very helpful. It was too clean, and I believe it was too clean because someone did a thorough cleaning either before or after Mrs. Comstock was murdered. I believe it is more evidence that the murder was not one of passion, but intentional and pre-meditated."

"So, all we have to do is find out who hated the woman enough to want her dead, and then carefully planned how to do it and make a clean get away?" Horace asked facetiously. "But wait a minute – it was Nine Fingers Charlie who did the deed."

Beatrix said slowly, "Perhaps, but I am not certain. There is something that does not make it quite as simple as we think. All we have to do is find the missing piece. We must take into consideration that Clarice and Harriet may have given us a new thread to follow. I think we might get even more information from Harriet."

Over dinner that evening Horace gently broached the question of who might have wanted to kill Mrs. Comstock. Harriet looked at him bleakly and said, "I can only tell you what I said before. There are a great number of people who feared and disliked her. I am sure many of us have muttered we wished she would just drop dead, but I can't imagine anyone actually pulling the trigger."

"And even fewer who would have the courage to do it," Clarice added. "Well, then again Miss Stymington and Mrs. Vandenberg are about as cold-blooded as they come, and they passionately hated Mrs. Comstock."

"Why?" Fred asked.

"The three of them move in the same circles, and they all play cards. They started out with whist, moved on to bridge, and now play Mah-jong. It's cutthroat, and rumor has it that they played for money. I think it is very low stakes because it is the prestige of winning that is important to them," Clarice said.

"Wait a minute, Clarice," Horace interrupted. "Whist, bridge, and Mah-jong require four plays. You mentioned only three. Who was the forth?"

"Usually it is Mrs. Gray. She moved here a few years ago, right after her husband died, because of Ox-Bow..." Clarice began.

"Oh, I know her. She has the gentlest disposition, and she is very generous," Harriet explained.

"The sad part of this is that the other three invite her to play because she is good at cards or tiles, but they are sometimes very rude to her. I don't know how to say it any better than this: She's part of their circle, but she's still something of an outsider, if that makes sense."

"It does to me!" Phoebe said. "There are girls like that in my class."

"Well, this is all very interesting, but I think we're getting off track with this," Horace said. "We need to stay focused."

"I know that Chief Garrison believes that Mr. Nine Fingers Charlie shot Old Curdle... I mean, shot Mrs. Comstock, but has he talked with Mr. Comstock? Maybe he has some ideas who did it," Phoebe said. The adults turned to look at her, realizing for the first time that everyone was so focused on Nine Fingers Charlie as the killer that they hadn't given much thought to Mr. Comstock.

"A very good point. Well done, Phoebs!" her grandfather said.

"Dr. Howell, may I see you for a moment, please?" Phoebe asked solemnly.

"Yes, of course! What is it?"

"I was at the Western Union when a news story about the Dole Air Race came over the wire. It was meant for the Commercial Record, but I read it. Are you familiar with it?" the girl asked.

"Yes, of course. Mr. Post suggested I should enter, but I chose against it. Why do you ask? Has the winner been announced, or is there bad news?" Beatrix asked.

"It's bad news. One of the planes is missing. It was flown by a Mildred Doran from here in Michigan. Did you know her?" Phoebe asked quietly.

"I knew of her, but I did not know her personally. She was very young to take such great risks. It is sad news, but not surprising. I have known for some time that she liked to fly and she was very courageous, but at her age, well, I question her experience flying over so much open water. I believe she preferred a Buhl Airsedan model, but I am not convinced that it is airworthy.

"Her plane is missing?" Beatrix asked again.

"Yes. There is a search going on but...."

"Thank you for telling me, Phoebe. If you learn anything more, please let me know. And Phoebe, one more thing. That was very thoughtful of you."

"I was thinking about you," Phoebe answered.

The comment startled Beatrix and confused her. She looked down and quietly said, "Oh. Thank you."

While the two of them were talking, Harriet was standing on the deck, leaning on the rail and looking at the river. Horace joined her. "I can understand why you love the water," she said quietly. "I think I sometimes take it for granted. Will you keep your boat forever?"

"Oh, I don't know. It's getting pretty old and takes a lot of repairs and routine maintenance. Captain G doesn't have much confidence about taking it out on the lake like we used to. We'll see. He said something odd. With a boat as old as this one, a lake is just one big grave carved out of water."

The quote made Harriet shudder in fear.

Horace continued. "I was thinking about Mrs. Comstock. Aside from being a pain in the gluteus maximus, medius and minimus, did she really sell many paintings? I mean, at her galleries in Chicago and St Louis, or out in New York?"

"I've sometimes wondered that. I really don't know. When it came to money and success sometimes I think she put on a big front. But, I really just don't know. If she had a good artist, then she made money, but if she couldn't sell a painting, then it was always because of the artist. A success was always because of her; a failure was someone else's fault. She was an absolute terror."

Harriet dropped her voice to a whisper and looked down at the deck. "I shouldn't think this way, but it's a relief that I won't have to deal with her anymore."

"I understand. I've heard that before. Come to think of it, I could probably say the same thing about some of my fellow physicians."

"Patients, too?" she asked.

"That would be breaking confidences," he chuckled.

"Looks to me like we got one last card to play and still need a few points to crib out," Fred said as he and Beatrix and Horace went for a twilight walk through town.

"I know you are speaking English, Fred, but I have no idea what you are saying," Beatrix told him.

"It means we are running out of clues and possibilities, and maybe one last chance to see this through to the end. If we can't make some progress with Mr. Comstock tomorrow or soon after, it might be game over," Horace explained.

"I see. Then we have no choice but to proceed," Beatrix answered glumly. "We need to work out a plan so we know what we are going to do. Besides, I have an extra ace up my sleeve."

FOURTEEN

"Fred, you just went past his driveway," Horace complained.

"I sure did done do that, Doc. I was down here the other day and a crew was working on the culvert up ahead. I want to see if the road is open or not. Might come in handy, if you know what I mean. Something to keep in mind for future reference," Fred answered. He continued down the lake road and saw that the construction was on-going, found a driveway, turned around, and returned to the Comstock home.

"Let us remember the plan," Beatrix said. "Horace and I will call on Mr. Comstock while you look around a bit and wait. Give us a couple of minutes, and then get out and just wander around. Fred, if anyone asks what you're doing, remember that you are just enjoying some fresh air while you wait."

"Got it," Fred replied. "All right, out you go."

"Mr. Comstock, my name is Horace Balfour and this is Doctor Beatrix Howell. We came to offer our condolences to you and your family," Horace said when the front door was opened by a thin greyish looking older man. Not surprisingly, he was nattily dressed in a three piece suit with a black armband.

"That is very kind of you. You were friends of Mrs. Comstock, were you?" he asked.

"I first met her as a student at Ox-Bow a couple of years ago and saw her from time to time," Beatrix explained.

"And you and I saw each other on a couple of occasions when you and Mrs. Comstock visited the art gallery that just opened," Horace added. He watched as Mr. Comstock winced. "As I said, we came to offer our condolences. You see, both of us are physicians and we know from experience how difficult things can be when a loved one dies suddenly and unexpectedly..."

"And tragically," Beatrix quickly added. She succeeded in not smiling as she watched Horace discreetly slide his foot between the door and frame. It was a trick he had learned many years ago when he made house calls to patients who were wary of a young physician. "Perhaps we could come inside for a minute or two," she suggested.

Mr. Comstock opened the door and said, "Yes, for a couple of minutes. I am not up for much company right now. That would be nice." He led the way into a large living room that over-looked the lake and motioned them toward a couple of side chairs.

"Were you also involved with the arts?" Horace asked.

Mr. Comstock tipped his head back and laughed. "No, that was my wife's hobby. I was, still am, an attorney. Well, I'm not as busy as I once was."

"A hobby you said. But I understand from Mrs. Waters at Ox-Bow that she had galleries in Chicago and St. Louis as well as one in Saugatuck. Surely that is more than a hobby."

He laughed again. "And, in New York City, too. No, it was a hobby. A very expensive hobby. The only way to lose money faster is to invest in live theatre or the talkies."

"I didn't realize that," Horace said softly. "I just assumed..."

"You're not alone. A lot of people think an art gallery, especially a good one, is a money-machine. Trust me, it isn't. No, her hobby cost me plenty, but she enjoyed it as long as she wasn't looking at the balance sheet. So, let's just say, I'll miss her, but not the big bills and the little income."

"I didn't know that. Well, we saw each other at the gallery in Saugatuck, but I was just the new boy, and the part time help, at that," Horace said. "I never saw the business end of it."

"Let me give you a little bit of advice you already know. Don't even think about it. Galleries, that is."

"Good advice. If ever I am tempted, I'll remember what you said. You know, one of the reasons we came out here was because it must seem discomforting that until the police find out who did it, everything isn't wrapped up..." Beatrix said, her voice trailing off as she stared out the window. "There is so much pain," she barely whispered.

"Very well phrased. Thank you," Mr. Comstock answered.

"Did you know anything about Nine Finger's Charlie? Well, outside of the times you saw him at the gallery," Horace asked.

Mr. Comstock paused before answering. "Well, only from what I read in the papers. He was a criminal, you know. I believe he was a safe-cracker and he targeted the homes of, of, well, the wealthy. I know he spent time in a penitentiary, but I don't think the police knew about all of his handy-work, so to speak."

"What do you mean?" Beatrix asked.

"From my experience, sometimes, when a very wealthy individual is burglarized, they don't want to report it. Too much notoriety, to begin with. Many times they do not want the embarrassment, nor all of the questions. We have our own ways of keeping secrets, just as I am sure physicians protect each other when there is malpractice," Mr. Comstock said.

Horace was about to make a retort, paused and thought better of it, and said, "No that is something we do not do. Each state has a medical board to look into allegations of wrong-doing or a death on the operating table."

"Be that as it may. Attorneys and physicians do not always do the same thing, nor the wealthy as the middle class," Mr. Comstock said icily. He stood up. "Thank you for calling and offering your condolences." He walked them to the door.

"Well, that was unpleasant, was it not?" Beatrix asked once she and Horace were in the car and Fred slid behind the wheel.

"Yes. Fred, any information?" Horace asked.

"There sure seems like something fishy is going on around here. I couldn't do much scouting because I saw someone behind the curtain in an upstairs room. I'm pretty sure I was being watched. But the rum thing is, there's a trail leading from the back door of the house, across the lawn, and to the carriage house. Back and forth, and as far as I can tell it's the only one. It's fresh, not heavy-worn from using it for a long time. Now, I didn't get a real close look-see, but from here I could see there's a big padlock on the door to the carriage house."

"That's odd, even if it does have a rational explanation," Beatrix said.

"Anything else?" Horace asked.

"No, sorry, Doc. Like I said I got the same feeling I was being watched like that times we were slipping through No Man's Land after dark. I figured I kept my head down then, and I'd better being doing it now."

"Very wise, Sergeant," Horace answered. "When we get back to the *Aurora* I'd like you to sketch it out for us. Nothing fancy. Just want to get a look at it on paper.

"Well, what do you make of our Mr. Lorenzo Comstock?" Beatrix asked as she settled into the leather chair in Horace's study.

"Without a baseline of his personality, it is hard to know," Horace said slowly, filling his pipe to give him more time to think. "It could be grief, or it could be that he was nervous because he had something to hide. He shut us down fast, but maybe it's because he wanted to be alone."

"Yes, but perhaps he is not accustomed to having anyone disagree with him or challenge his opinions. The other thing is that Fred said he thought he was being watched from an upstairs window. Assuming that he was correct, perhaps Mr. Comstock was in some type of danger and wanted to get us out the door quickly," Beatrix suggested.

"Or, perhaps he had something else to hide. You said something the other evening about Nine Fingers Charlie having a number of aliases."

"Yes," Beatrix paused, then smiled. "I trust you reread some of the clippings a second time. There were at least five different names, perhaps more. We know Nine Fingers Charlie had a number of aliases, and we just heard Mr. Comstock strongly hinting that a number of safes must have been burgled, but no one wanted to say anything."

"That's what I think, too. But the question is 'why'? Why, if someone had money or jewelry or anything else stolen from their safe wouldn't they make a report to the police? It has to be more than embarrassment."

"It does not seem logical," Beatrix objected. "It is as if they have something much larger to hide."

"No, it isn't logical," Horace agreed. "At least not yet. There must be some more missing pieces to all of this. But what were they *really* trying to hide?"

The two of them sat in silence, thinking it through. "All right, Beatrix. Time to get on our feet and go for a walk. A change of scenery might help. Besides, I've got something to show you. Horace stood up and waited for Beatrix to get out of the chair.

"Horace, please tell me we are not going to Parrish's for another one of those horrible Green River soda drinks," she said.

"No. Not a bad idea, though. No. This is something different. Now, if you like, we could stop by the soda fountain on the way back..." Horace teased.

"Nor for coffee and donuts at the Princess," she said.

"Too early in the day for that."

"You brought me to see some carpenters at work?" Beatrix asked.

"Not quite. This is one of those new houses from Sears Roebuck. They make everything at a factory, put it into a boxcar and send it to anywhere in the country. Every board cut and ready, every nail supplied. All the pipes for water and all the wire for electricity!"

"I see," Beatrix said quietly. "Well, at least it is a nice day for a short walk."

"You don't sound very excited about it. It's the engineering, and because everything is brought here to be assembled, it saves a fortune. More people can afford to buy their own home. And, it saves time, which means someone can move into their home that much faster." He led her over to a work table covered with the blue prints and some pictures. Even after she looked at them, she was still not impressed.

"I was under the impression we were going to think about the murder," she said quietly.

"We are. Remember how Sherlock Holmes would do something entirely different and then come up with a solution?"

"Yes."

"Well, that's what we're doing right now. Something entirely different, and perhaps we will come up with a solution."

"Perhaps we would be better off if we had coffee and a donut," Beatrix said flatly.

"Or, a Green River."

"No." Beatrix looked at her watch. "Aren't you supposed to report for duty at the hospital, Doctor?"

FIFTEEN

"I have been thinking about our highly unusual conversation with Mr. Comstock," Beatrix said when Horace returned from his afternoon at the hospital.

"And hello to you, too," Horace said.

"Oh, yes. Hello. I was focused on the murder. Hello. Again," she said abruptly. "I have been thinking about our highly unusual conversation with Mr. Comstock," Beatrix repeated. "I found it exceptionally awkward. He was too guarded."

"Yes?"

"Therefore, I charted out what you were working on, she said, handing him sheets of typing paper with notes. "My work from this afternoon; on the top row, the names of all the people associated with the murder – Nine Fingers, Mrs. Comstock, and so on...."

Horace interrupted. "These two – Flopsy and Mopsy. Who are they?"

Beatrix smiled. "Those are your two flappers."

"I'd prefer to forget about them," Horace replied.

Beatrix ignored him and continued, explaining that beneath each person she had listed all of the facts and information they had collected. "And on the next pages, and in the same order, I have written all of the rumors, stories, and speculations on each of them. In short, everything of which I could think. As you can see, we have considerable information about Nine Fingers Charlie. After him, we start having less and less information. We know of Mrs. Comstock's galleries, as well as Mr. Comstock's comments that they were not profitable. That is not verified, by the way. But we have nothing about Mr. Comstock except that he was a railroad attorney, but several different lines have been mentioned. There is nothing except for the nicknames of the two flappers who may or may not have anything to do with the murder."

"Can't we leave those two out of this? They were a couple of holiday-makers here for a day or two," Horace objected again.

Beatrix looked over her glasses at him, making it clear her answer was 'no'.

She continued. "Because we have so much information about Nine Fingers Charlie, and because we have very good reason to believe he may be a criminal, and because he is absent, we are jumping to the conclusion that he killed Mrs. Comstock. That may be in error."

"Yes, well Mrs. Comstock was found shot to death in his shop, the building locked, he has the only key, and he is missing, so it's a safe assumption," Horace objected.

"I would normally agree with you, but Harriet and Clarice mentioned two women from town who despised her."

"Beatrix, that's a bit thin, don't you think?" Horace asked. "First of all, what motive would they have to kill her? Second, how would someone other than Nine Fingers Charlie get into the gallery? It was locked. And how would they persuade Mrs. Comstock to come into town at night, get her into the gallery, shoot her, and then get away, oh, and lock the door before they left?"

"Yes, it would be a challenge, but not an insurmountable one. I doubt that you and Fred are the only two people in Saugatuck who are proficient at picking locks. Clarice and I believe we have a plan that may work. We shall find out tomorrow afternoon."

"Beatrix, I know you told me you knew how to play whist, but *just when* did you last play?" Clarice asked as they relaxed on two deck chairs after their guests had left.

"My third year of college, the winter term. At Christmastime, during the holidays, Mother thought it might be a pleasurable diversion and improve my non-existent social life. It did neither. I believe that when I returned to school, sometime in late January, was the last time I played until this afternoon."

"But that's nearly...." Clarice started to say.

"Yes, thank you. It was a long time ago and there is no need to review statistics. I proposed whist rather than bridge because it is something all of us would have played before bridge became so popular," Beatrix interrupted.

"How clever of you! I warned you they could be ruthless."

"Yes. That observation was confirmed when Miss Stymington offered her cards, and I noticed they were marked," Beatrix said with a slight lilt to her voice.

"What?" Clarice asked.

"Yes. I noticed they are marked. I saw four circles near the top and the bottom on the front of the cards when we were cutting for seating rights and fortunately, Miss Stymington and I were partners. Each circle was divided by twelve points. There was a small dot at the end of the line signifying the number on the card in that suit. An ace was marked with a small dot in the middle of the circle. I knew the cards I was holding and could read the cards in Miss Stymington's hands. After that, all I had to do was remember which cards you and Mrs. Vandenberg been played. It was rather simple, really," Beatrix said.

"Well, it certainly had Miss Symington flustered."

"Yes, and that was my intention. She could not see the cards you and Mrs. Vandenberg were holding because you were sitting to her side, and I kept mine covered. By the time we paused after the third game I believe she was somewhat perplexed. I am sure you noticed she drained her wine glass very quickly," Beatrix said flatly, almost as if she was giving a medical report.

"So, that's why you suddenly brought up the Comstock Murder Case!" Clarice laughed with delight. "Brilliant work. Now, what's the next step?"

"We wait and see. We may have unnerved Mrs. Vandenberg and Miss Stymington, but that is no reason to believe that they cannot regain their composure. Or, perhaps our bluff worked and they may confess. We must also keep in mind that they may have nothing to confess. We lit the fuse; let us see what may come of it. We can only hope that it will be of some help."

Beatrix waited impatiently for Horace to return to the boat from his afternoon at the hospital. "You told me this morning that Fred has some connection with some, shall we say gentlemen of shady reputation, who reacted to the name of Nine Fingers Charlie, and that you hope to see them this evening. That will be beneficial."

"If they talk," Horace cautioned. "And, if they are there."

"That is why I believe I should be there. I believe your reputation of being a gentleman would be enhanced if you escort me, rather than leave the impression that you are some sort of Stage Door Johnny or sugar daddy, as they are sometimes called, who consorts with flappers."

"You're coming along with Fred and me?" Horace asked.

"Yes. And while you were at the hospital Clarice and I spent the afternoon playing whist with Mrs. Vandenberg and Miss Stymington. I believe we may have flushed them out, if only a little."

Horace looked at her blankly, confused. "How did you do that?"

Beatrix gave a slight smile. "I cheated."

"You did what?" Horace asked.

"I cheated. I simply did what I instantly realized was Miss Stymington's original intention. I merely did it before she had the opportunity."

"Why? Why would you do that?" Horace asked.

"I wanted to see her true nature, as well as how she would react when challenged. I must think about it further, but there is a true possibility she has it within her to have killed Mrs. Comstock if she was sufficiently provoked. Now, we must set that aside and focus on talking with Fred's acquaintances,"

The three men from the night before were once again sitting at the same table near the sidewall of the Big Pavilion. Fred sauntered over with Horace and Beatrix behind him. The two of them were reeling from the loud music and even larger crowd. It didn't seem to bother Fred, and after the usual round of greetings, he made the introductions "My boss worked for Nine Fingers, and wants to get paid for his time. It's a matter of honor and respect."

A grizzled short, thin man stood up, realized Beatrix was present and removed his fedora and put out his hand. "Thomas McChesney, but everyone calls me 'Lug. Lug Wrench'. So, you worked for Nine Fingers and he stiffed you, huh?"

"Sort of looks that way. I heard he's on the run," Horace said glumly. "So, maybe there's not much chance of getting my money, is there?"

"Yeah, we were just talking about him. He's slippery, that one. But say, it's not his style to use a gun. I didn't think he even had one, much less knew how to use it. No idea what got into him. And you're right – not much chance of getting your money out of him, 'specially if he's dead somewhere from being caught on the business end of a piece."

"Nor a lug wrench, huh, Lugs?" one of his friends laughed, punching him in the shoulder. He turned to Horace, Fred, and Beatrix. "You're right. Nine Fingers wasn't the rough sort of guy. His specialty is cracking a safe, and he didn't need dynamite to do it, either."

"What do you mean, Mr. Wrench?" Beatrix asked.

"Mr. Wrench?" He laughed, "Now that's a good one, and don't you boys get any ideas about repeating it," he warned his friends. "What I mean is that when he was doing a job he had the touch. Soft sensitive fingers so he could feel the tumblers drop. Real patient, like, and quiet. And fast. Say, he could be fast on a three tumbler safe. He was a legend. He liked those. Tumblers would drop, he'd pull down on the handle and scoop out whatever was inside, and be gone out the door in no time."

For a few minutes the three men regaled Horace, Beatrix, and Fred with stories about Nine Fingers Charlie's alleged successes and the colossal failure of other less skill crooks.

"The thing about Nine Fingers is that he was a specialist. Nothing he liked better than cracking a four tumbler Mosher safe that belonged to a lawyer, and not just any lawyer, but a railroad one," Lug explained. "I'll tell you one thing, I never saw Nine Fingers Charlie have it in for no one, nicest guy around, but you bring up a railroad lawyer, and hey, he'd go right off the rails."

Fred burst out laughing. "That's a good one. Railroad lawyer sent him right off the rails!" He looked across the table and notice Beatrix was staring blankly at him.

She quickly interrupted. "Why a four tumbler Mosher safe?"

"Well, see with four tumblers it's more of a challenge, and that's what Nine Fingers liked – a challenge. Besides, those train lawyers thought they were pretty smart, you know, law school and all. Three tumblers wasn't good enough for them, but they got suckered in on believing no one could break a four," one of the men explained.

"Any idea why he had it in for railroad lawyers?" Horace asked.

"Sure. I know plenty about that. The truth of the matter was that Nine Fingers came from South Dakota. Yankton, I think. Well, somewhere out there. And see, the railroads were gouging the farmers and ranchers out west where he come from, and the lawyers were crooked ones who made it possible. You know how old Frank and Jesse James robbed banks and trains to give the money to the poor? Well, that was Nine Fingers Charlie doing the same to the real crooks – the lawyers," one of the men said. Everyone at the table laughed.

"Ah," Lugs objected, "that's a lot of hooey and a fancy story, and you know it. My money is on some lawyer telling Nine Finger that he wasn't good enough to ask his daughter to step out with him. It makes sense, too. A man doesn't want to advertise stuff like that, so he created that whopper of a story to make hisself look good.

"Do you gentlemen know what Nine Fingers Charlie did with all his money?" Beatrix asked.

"Nope. Never heard nothing about that, and if Charlie wasn't going to say something then we weren't going to pry into his business," Lugs answered.

"Say, back to business for a minute," Horace interrupted. "I came here hoping you could help me find Nine Fingers Charlie because he owed me some money. You sure you don't know where he is?" Horace asked.

"Sure wish we could help you out, but I figure if he plugged that woman through the heart, he's not hanging around town to give you some pocket change. He's long gone and working on the next job by now," Lugs said.

"Not exactly the news I wanted to hear. And, you're sure he shot that woman, I take it. Say, listen fellows, we've taken up enough of your time, and we ought to be on our way. Thanks for your help," Horace said as he stood up to shake hands all around before they left.

"Thank goodness we are out there," Beatrix said. "It was so noisy."

"I agree," Horace said. "Why don't we go somewhere quiet and talk for a while, and see if we can figure this out."

"Say, the drug store might still be open if you're thinking about a Green River," Fred suggested.

"I will come along as long as I do not have to have one of those hideous phosphates," Beatrix said softly. "Some ice cream and chocolate sauce will suffice."

The waitress took their order, and while they waited Horace asked, "Well, any ideas or thoughts?"

"It appears to me that Nine Fingers Charlie is something of a chameleon and held in high repute by his fellow criminals," Beatrix said. "Even so, I cannot help but question the veracity of their stories, and at the same time wonder if they may know more about his whereabouts than they are letting on."

"Seems like he's some sort of modern day Robin Hood, the way they were talking about him, Fred said.

"With a dash of the Scarlet Pimpernel," Beatrix added. "However, we have no idea what he did with the money he was taking from these safes. At the moment, I have no idea if what the three men said is of help or hindrance."

They were silent while the waitress brought their desserts, and then Horace said, "Well, Beatrix, let's read through those newspaper clippings again and see if any of it connects with Nine Fingers Charlie. Maybe we'll pick up something more to be added to your charts, huh?" He paused, then added, "It might be a long night. I'd better get you a couple more cigars and matches."

Beatrix let out a long sigh. "I have my doubts it will get us anywhere, but you are right, it is best to go over it all once again."

SIXTEEN

"Clarice told me that you're quite the card shark," Theo said to Beatrix as he carried his coffee to join the two of them in Horace's study.

"Thank you," she said quietly. "It troubles me that I was forced to take advantage of the situation like that."

"Yes, but for a good cause," Horace told her.

"Yes, I know you are right, and I did force her to show her true colors," she replied.

"What do you mean?" Theo asked. "You mean, you weren't playing for money?"

Beatrix gasped in horror. "The woman came with the intention of winning which was true for all of us. But she came prepared to cheat if necessary. That is unacceptable. What troubles me is that I lowered myself, my standards, really, to her level."

"I understand, but it was for a good cause," Horace repeated, this time with more emphasis. "Now, more importantly, what did you learn about them? Anything that might be a clue to solving this murder?"

"I believe so. Miss Stymington and Mrs. Vandenberg were already highly competitive before starting our card game. When Miss Stymington and I became partners, I believe it was her intention not only to win, but to take the most tricks. I did not allow that to happen, and it was very challenging for her to accept," Beatrix explained. "She was not a woman accustomed to losing."

"All right, so you were partners, but you were competing against her," Theo said, confused.

"Yes, and that is when both women began to show their true colors, as I just said. Mrs. Vandenberg realized what was happening to Miss Stymington, that she was losing, and began making some very snide comments to her about her poor performance. Suffice it to say that it did not go unchallenged."

"Thunderation, just what did you learn from all of this?" Horace asked.

"That the two women are, as I said, highly competitive. Picture them as two snarling, hissing cats, their claws out, ready to assert their dominance. I believe they jealously compete over everything in their lives, as proven by a very simple card game. Miss Stymington did not like being shown up as second best to me; Mrs. Vandenberg lost no opportunity to provoke and needle her. Now, if they behaved and spoke this way over a mere past-time, you can well imagine what they are like with something more significant."

"All right, I get the picture. The question remains: Would one or both of them have killed Mrs. Comstock?" Horace asked.

Beatrix looked at the Balfour brothers blankly and said quietly, "I don't know." The two remained silent, giving her time to explain.

"As unpleasant as this petty jealousy might be, I believe that they truly enjoy it, otherwise they would have brought it to an end. Instead, they goaded each other. Perhaps it has been going on for such a long that they don't know any other way to act and speak. In some ways, it almost gives them something to do."

"Now there's a wasted life for you! Thunderation!" Horace barked.

"I agree," Beatrix said. "And yet, they seem to live very confined lives that revolve around social gatherings and committee meetings. That, in my opinion, a calendar filled with such events, would be a wasted life. If I am right about this, then their behavior gives them some excitement. If that is the case, they need each other as adversaries, so it would be very unlikely that they would murder one of their own. To do so would be counterproductive.

"At the same time, it appears that Mrs. Comstock was more of an outsider associated with the other women. She and her husband have a home here, but it is several miles away, and they are here only part-time in the summer. There are any number of reasons why one or both of the women might have wanted her dead. She might be too assertive and threatening, for example. Think of it as Elizabeth of England killing her rival Mary of Scotland."

"This sounds more like the gangsters in Chicago and New York City," Horace muttered in disgust.

"Indeed. Only in this case, instead of hard currency it is social currency," Beatrix told him.

"All right, you two. Is this getting us anywhere?" Theo asked.

"Only that we know it is very possible one or both of them could be capable of murder," Beatrix said firmly.

Theo was frustrated at a lack of firm answers and changed the subject. "Did you three learn anything last night when you were at the Big Pavilion?"

"Only that Fred knows some very interesting characters," Horace answered, almost flippantly. "Plus some anecdotes and tall tales about Nine Fingers Charlie's past. I'm not certain if it is mainly myth, or if those fellows were playing us for fools, I think they were having a good laugh at our expense."

"The general opinion is that Nine Fingers Charlie shot Mrs. Comstock and by now he is long gone. That said, their story could be pure fiction as they could be covering for him, or even hiding him," Beatrix said. "When we returned from the Big Pavilion we spent several hours re-reading the newspaper accounts of him, and he certainly is a chameleon. All of which means he could be in town or long gone; he could have shot Mrs. Comstock, the vicious ladies could have shot her, or... someone else."

"Beatrix, is there any chance you might get a different perspective it you took your plane up?" Theo asked.

"I had considered that as a possibility. However, when we drove there I noticed the trees are so thick that there is very little that could be seen from the air. At best, it would only attract unwanted attention."

"Thunderation! Look, Beatrix, you flushed out those two women, we tried getting something out of the fellows last night; now who are we missing?" Horace snapped.

She stared blankly at Horace and finally said, "I am not even certain anymore."

"Well, Chief Garrison has already grilled the two women who work in Mrs. Comstock's gallery. Both of them have solid alibis for that night. Besides, without her around they're going to be out of a job," Theo said. "They're going to be out of a job anyway because Mr. Comstock told them he's closing the place."

"Maybe they have other jobs lined up so being out of work doesn't matter. What about the other gallery owners? With her out of the way, that's less competition and more customers. Do either of you know if the chief talked to them?" Horace asked.

"If he has, he did not mention it," Theo answered.

"Oh, my. I do not like the fact that we are as short-sighted as the chief," Beatrix said quietly. "That is very embarrassing." She suddenly stood up. "Stop. Not another word for a moment, please!

Horace, some paper and a pen, please." He handed a notebook and pen, and they all waited for her to jot down some notes. "Proceed, gentlemen."

"Yeah, it is. So, let's go talk to the other owners, find out what they thought of Mrs. Comstock, and see if they know anyone who had a grudge against her," Theo said.

"Slow down," Horace said. "There's a short cut. Instead of running around town to every gallery, let's narrow it down by talking with Bobbie over to the telephone office. No one knows better than she what's going on in Saugatuck."

"You going?" Theo asked.

"Nope. This is a job for our spy. We'll send Phoebe. Look, she wants to help, and talking with Bobbie is about a safe a job as we could give her." He pulled out his pocket watch. "She should be here by now."

"Phoebs, we need your help solving this case," her grandfather began. For the next few minutes Horace, Theo, and Beatrix explained the assignment to her. To Horace's delight, she was beaming.

"Looks like you're ready for your first real assignment. Now, take along some paper and a pencil, and just as soon as you finish, and don't forget to thank her, go over to the park and write down everything you learned."

"Got it!" she said brightly.

"You think I ought to go along and keep watch? You know, keep an eye on the place while she's in there and then while she's at the park?" Fred asked.

"Thank you for the offer, Sergeant, but I think Phoebs will be perfectly safe. Do you agree, or would you be more comfortable if Fred stood sentry duty?"

"Thank you, Fred," she said, then paused. "You know, I would like a body guard."

Her decision surprised Horace. As they were leaving his study Horace asked Phoebe to wait a moment. "You sure you're okay doing this?" he asked.

"Oh, of course. I asked Fred to come along because I know what it's like to be left out. I didn't want him to feel he wasn't needed."

Horace swallowed hard and barely croaked out, "I see" before he nodded toward the door. The girl had a far bigger heart than any one of them.

"I won't say 'no' if you are offering," Beatrix said wearily, holding two fingers up and slightly apart. Horace smiled, turned to remove a bottle from the cabinet behind his desk, and then handed her a cigar after he had poured her a drink.

"Long day at the office?" he said, trying to lighten the mood. She ignored the comment.

"Horace, I trust you realize we are going backwards. We continue to add more names. Miss Stymington and Mrs. Vandenberg from this afternoon. Now, it's the two women who worked in Mrs. Comstock's gallery, and all of the other gallery owners. I believe the general practice is to start excluding names, not adding more. This has to stop or we'll suspect everyone in town."

They sat in silence for a few minutes until Horace asked, "Who do you think did it?"

Beatrix had a far-away look in her eyes as she answered, "As unlikely as it may seem, Miss Stymington and Mrs. Vandenberg are at the top of my list, either jointly or separately."

"How do you figure that?" Horace asked, lighting his pipe once again.

"We just added several more names, and it is possible they might have done it, but I seriously doubt they had the ability to put a plan together. They are too young and inexperienced. If she had been murdered in her own shop, it might be the result of a moment of passion. This was not. It was a cold, calculating plan. From what I saw of Miss Stymington, she has the right personality to plan a murder and kill someone in cold blood."

Horace's eyes widened in surprise. "But what about Nine Fingers Charlie? It's possible he came to Saugatuck to open a gallery with the intent of shooting Mrs. Comstock, don't you think?"

"No," Beatrix said flatly, finishing her drink. "First, from what you and Fred's friends, that Mr. Lug Wrench, for example, he did not have the personality of a killer. Second, he went to tremendous effort to open a shop just so he could shoot her. There would have been endless possibilities to do it elsewhere. For example, when she was driving to and from her home, or even at her home."

"A refill?" Horace offered, then continued. "Why those two?

"If someone is so desperate to win a simple, meaningless, little game of whist, then there is no limit to what that person might do if challenged by a real opponent," Beatrix said.

SEVENTEEN

An hour or so later, Horace watched as his granddaughter came up the gangplank of the *Aurora*. Fred pulled up moments later, having trailed behind her to make sure she wasn't being followed. "Phoebs, please tell us you have some good, solid information from your talk with Bobbie," Horace told his granddaughter. He motioned toward his study. "We could use a break about now. Say, before you start, see if your uncle Theo is anywhere nearby."

She returned with him and Fred.

"To answer your question: Well, yes and no. Maybe. I guess I really don't know. Bobbie and I talked, and she said that no one in town really liked Mrs. Comstock, but there wasn't anyone who would have wanted to shoot and kill her because she was what Bobbie called 'a source of amusement,'" Phoebe said.

"Source of amusement? You might have to explain that one," Theo said.

"I had to ask Bobbie, too. Here's pretty much what she said," Phoebe explained, pulling out her note- pad and looking at her notes. "Everyone thought she was pretty snooty. You know, nose up in the air so she could look down on everyone. She would tell everyone she had a trained eye for art, that she knew good stuff from bad, things like that, and was always talking about her galleries in New York and places like that. .She constantly criticized new artists, always finding something wrong and never had a nice thing say to them until their paintings started selling. She liked them as long as their paintings were selling, but the minute they weren't, they were out the door. And, the other gallery owners had lots of stories about customers who had gone to her gallery and been insulted and said they would never go back."

"Anything more?" Horace asked.

Phoebe closed her notebook and looked at her grandfather. "No. That was about it. She said the same thing three different ways. Was I of any help?"

"Yes, Phoebe, you were," Beatrix told her. "You confirmed what we already suspected. It is very helpful to get the same message from someone outside the social or art circles. You did a good piece of detective work.

Remembering Phoebe's concern for including Fred, Horace asked, "Any sign of trouble while you were watching out for my granddaughter?" Just as he expected, there was none.

After Phoebe gave her report they were quiet for a while, thinking it over, until Theo said, "And that means we're at a dead end. Like you said, Horace, it reconfirms everyone and everything else. That's that." Fred agreed, and the two men and Phoebe filtered out of the study, leaving Beatrix behind with Horace.

"I doubt that Chief Garrison will be interested in what Phoebe found out, or in what I learned playing cards with Miss Stymington and Mrs. Vandenberg. It appears he wants to make it a straight line to Nine Fingers Charlie, does it not?" She paused to look off into the distance. "If you're offering I will help you violate the Volstead Act again."

"With a cigar, too?" Horace asked.

"With a cigar."

They sat in silence, lost in their own thoughts, distracted by the curl of smoke drifting up from her cigar and his pipe. "Let's go for a drive this evening," Horace suggested.

"Yes. It would be pleasant, but why? To what ends?"

"Just a mental diversion. Perhaps we'll see things from a different perspective," he said lightly. "Of course, if you'd rather not, we could always go for a walk and see how the construction is coming on that new house."

"No thank you. I would prefer to go for a drive," she told him. "Horace, I can not understand why you are so interested in seeing a house being built. Surely, you must have seen other houses being built."

"In that case, a drive it is. We'll go after dinner. Maybe see how the crops are coming along," he said brightly.

"The crops? Well, at least it will be an improvement on looking at a house being built," Beatrix said. She paused, then added, "Please tell me you have not heard of a barn-raising happening tonight?"

"No. That generally happens during the daytime. But, if we do see one, we can always lend a hand," he teased. "I had no idea you were so interested in barn-raisings."

Beatrix looked at him blankly, finished her Scotch, and left his study.

For once, Horace didn't mind being on his own. He got up from behind his desk to lock the door, then filled his pipe and lit it. The pouch, matches, and a spare pipe were on his desk.

Just before Mrs. Garwood rang the first gong for dinner, Theo knocked on the study door. "I know you're in there," he said when

Horace didn't answer. Reluctantly, Horace unlocked the door and let us brother come in.

"You've been thinking. It smells like you've been burning your old socks. I can tell from the way my eyes are burning," Theo said.

"I have. Been thinking, that is. Beatrix and I are going for a drive this evening."

"Oh. I was thinking you two might like to see a new film with us at the Big Pavilion tonight."

"I appreciate the offer, but I just asked Beatrix if she'd like to go out in the country."

"Just asked? That was more like a couple of hours ago. What's going on in that brain of yours? I can see the little wheels are turning," Theo asked.

"Well, I've been turning this murder over in my mind. The other day when we drove down to the Comstock place Fred was pretty certain that he was being watched. Now, if it was anyone but Fred I'd write it off as just a case of the jitters, but the old sergeant's pretty level headed. Meanwhile, I've got Beatrix thinking that maybe Mrs. Vandenberg or Miss Stymington, or the two of them killed Mrs. Comstock," Horace said.

"They can't both be right, you know," Theo said.

"That's exactly what I thought at first. But, now hear me out on this before you say anything; but what if Miss Stymington had, still has, designs on Mr. Comstock? Thunderation, she's as competitive as they come. What if she started setting her cap for him, just to score another little victory over Mrs. C? And what if Comstock encouraged her? Look, I saw him hanging back when she stormed into Nine Finger's gallery, looking like a whipped dog...." Horace's voice trailed off.

"A crime of passion? No, you can't be right about that. Look, Miss Stymington and Mrs. Comstock were too much alike. No man in his right mind would be that foolish.

"Say, you remember telling me about those two flappers who came into the gallery, and how they needed to get out the back door when the Comstocks were about to come in? I'd sooner put my money on some funny business between him and those two young women than I would on Miss Stymington," Theo retorted.

"Maybe. But not is there is a lot of money thrown in the mix. Don't forget, Comstock was losing money on his wife's galleries. No telling what might happen when there's big money involved," Horace answered. "Anyway, Beatrix and I are going for a ride and who knows, maybe we'll get lucky."

"Do you think you'll achieve anything?" Theo asked.

"Thunderation! I've been sitting in the waiting room long enough. Chief Garrison is out looking for Nine Fingers, running around like a chicken with its head cut off and getting nowhere, and we're not doing much better! We'll go out for a ride and swing by the Comstock place. That's all I know!"

Neither of the Balfour brothers had seen Beatrix in the doorway of the study.

"You realize that will take us right past the Comstock house, do you not? Or was that what you had in mind?"

"You must be clairvoyant," Horace chuckled.

"Not in this case. Just an elementary and logical deduction, Sherlock," she teased back. "Still, you are right. There is something about the house and compound that is very off-putting. I realize that Mr. Comstock may still be suffering from grief and shock, but it is abnormal. Horace, you and Theo have had patients that died and grieving families, and some of them behave oddly, but there is something that is not right about this."

Horace said, "What I can't figure out is why Chief Garrison hasn't questioned him? He got his statement, but he hasn't follow through."

"Perhaps he was afraid that it would cause Mr. Comstock more pain and suffering just after his wife was killed. Plus, he is convinced that Nine Fingers Charlie is the killer. Figuring that out is simple.

"And since when did our chief ever care about someone other than himself?" Horace retorted.

"It is more than Mr. Comstock's behavior when we were at his house. There are hidden secrets. Fred thought he was being watched from an upstairs window..."

Horace interrupted, "If Fred thought he was being watched, my money is on the fact he was being watched. Sorry, go ahead, Beatrix."

"Plus, he said he could see that trail in the grass going out to the carriage house. That could be someone carrying items out to the building, however. You are right, it warrants another look," she continued.

"Well, let's see if we can get Fred to come along. Theo, too. We'll drive down there just a little before dusk, slow down at that bend just before we get to the Comstock place so Fred can jump out of the car. Then, he cuts through the woods so he can watch the front door of the carriage house and the front door of the main house. If it's all quiet, he can move in a bit closer and find out if there is something else going on.

"Once we drop Fred off, then we drive on down along the road like we're looking at the sunset over the lake. We pull over and watch the sun go down, and then turn around. By then, Fred can see our headlights. He'll meet us right where we dropped him off, pick him up, and come back." Horace smiled, quite pleased with himself.

Let me take one guess: we will be back just in time for a Green River before the drug store closes, will we not?"

"Did I say anything about a Green River?" he teased.

Their plans went awry right from the start. After dinner, about a half an hour before sunset, Horace and Beatrix met Fred at the car. "Fred, you'll need to get out on the left side, so take the back seat, left side, please. Beatrix, up front with me. I trust you have your have your equalizer with you?"

"Sure do." He pulled a set of brass knuckles out of his jacket pocket, and produced a short thick wooden dowel from the waistband of his trousers.

"Those knuckle dusters I understand, but why that odd looking billy club?" Beatrix wanted to know.

"Oh, that there isn't no ordinary billy club, Doc. Miss Phoebe's fellow, Henry, I think that's the one she's sweet on right now, must have wanted to get in good with me, so he gave me this genuine Michigan-made northern pike fish bat. Now, you hook one of those big northern on your line and he'll put up a fight, which is all right. But then, if you don't whack him a good one, once he gets in the boat, he'll thrash around and bite you with them sharp teeth, and that isn't so much fun. One good whack, and the next stop is the frying pan. So, I figured it might come in handy tonight, if you get my drift," Fred explained.

Before either Horace or Beatrix could say anything more Phoebe came running down the gangplank. "Grandfather! You promised to give me a driving lesson, remember?"

"Your grandfather did, but this is not the right time. We must take a drive down along the lake, and it will be after dark before we get back," Beatrix told her.

"Then I can practice my driving after dark!" Phoebe chirped, knowing she might yet win this debate.

"You know, all things considered, allowing Phoebe to drive us down there might be a good idea," Beatrix said, abruptly having changed her mind. "Yes, I think it would be a good idea. But you must promise to drive slowly. There might be people out for an evening stroll, or perhaps animals on the road."

Beatrix looked at Horace, winked, and slowly drew her index finger along the right side of her nose. Finally, he understood her plans and nodded in agreement.

"How would you like me to be your teacher tonight?" she asked. Phoebe gave her a big smile.

When they were still a hundred yards from the Comstock house, right at the last bend of the road that would obscure their view, Beatrix told Phoebe to slow down and stop. To the girl's surprise, Fred jumped out and closed the door. "Good hunting, Sergeant," Horace told him.

He gave a quick salute and added, "See you back here a little at the rendezvous point after sunset, Sir," then darted behind some shrubs.

"Go ahead, Phoebe," Beatrix whispered, "and take your time. We can enjoy looking at the houses and scenery. It is beautiful this time of the evening, is it not? Has your mother ever explained the Golden Hour to you?"

"No," the girl answered warily, still confused about what was happening.

"It is the hour before sunset, when the sun is low on the horizon. That changes the angle of the light rays, and the color of everything it strikes. We're too late today, but this time tomorrow you will see how different everything looks from just a few minutes earlier. Please slow down a little more so we can enjoy the beauty."

Realizing that Beatrix was trying to keep Phoebe distracted so she wouldn't ask too many questions, Horace joined in. "You know, there's an easy way to tell how soon the sun will set."

"Besides a clock?" the girl asked.

"Yes. I learned this on a canoe trip in northern Wisconsin. You hold your arm out, turn your hand so your fingers are horizontal, line them up on the horizon, and count the number of fingers from the bottom m edge of the sun to the horizon. Every finger is just about fifteen minutes, so four fingers would be an hour. I'll show you how to do it in the next day or so," Horace promised.

They passed the Comstock home, giving anyone inside sufficient opportunity to see Doctor Horace's big LaSalle as it passed. Horace planned on waving, and if he seemed encouraging, he'd have Phoebe come to a stop so he could talk with Mr. Comstock. He hoped that if someone saw the car they might not notice Fred moving through the woods toward their carriage house.

Beatrix continued. "Have you ever heard of the Green Flash?"

"The Green Flash? No. What is it?"

"Just at sunset, just as soon as the sun goes below the horizon, if it is a clear night over the lake, absolutely clear, for a second or two there is a flash of green from some of the last rays of the sun. I doubt we'll see it tonight because there is a cloud bank to the west."

They drove slowly south along the lake road, enjoying the view until Phoebe commented. "Oh – oh, someone must be in a hurry," as she glanced in the rear view mirror. Horace turned around to look. "It's Comstock's car. Beatrix, we've got company on our tail feathers."

"That is not good, is it?" she asked.

"No," Horace said quietly. He pulled down the dump seat in front of him and reached into the pouch. "Beatrix, better take this," he said as he handed her a small revolver,

"Thank you, Horace, but I prefer my own. Phoebe, speed up!" she said urgently.

"I hate telling you this, but the culvert is still out. We're going to run out of road before long," Horace said urgently.

"Then we must not let that happen," Beatrix said calmly. She turned to Phoebe and said, "Do you remember what I told you to do if you are being followed? Think through each of the steps, then tell me what you are going to do."

"Accelerate, then clutch in, shift down to second. Slam on the brakes and turn hard to the left. Then let the clutch out and press down hard on the accelerator. Speed up and maintain control."

"Very good. Now, accelerate. I will tell you when to do it."

"They're gaining on us!" Horace said.

"Phoebe! Now!"

Horace was thrown across the seat, sliding from the right side and slamming into the left door. "Thunderation! What are you doing, girl?" he demanded as he righted himself.

"It worked!" Phoebe shouted with joy, almost as if she had forgotten a few times when she had practiced it. They whizzed past the Comstock car, then their house, and headed back towards Saugatuck.

"It is called a Bootlegger's Turn. It is very effective, is it not? I taught her," Beatrix calmly said with pride.

Horace looked out the rear window. "They're turning around again. Thunderation girl, get some speed up so we can outrun them. Head straight into town and to the police station. Whatever they want, they won't follow us there."

The two women ignored him.

"What about Fred?" Phoebe asked.

"He knows how to look after himself. Fred's a tough old soldier, and he'll know what to do," Horace told her.

Beatrix asked Phoebe quietly. "Do you think you can do the turn again?"

"Sure! That was fun!" Phoebe laughed.

"Thunderation! It's not fun back here. At least you can hold on to the steering wheel!"

"Then I would suggest you hold on to something tight the next time," Beatrix said. "Phoebe, slow down a little and let them get a bit closer. They will not expect you to do it a second time. Let them get closer so we can put a stop to this game."

"A few more seconds. Wait for a wider spot in the road. There! Now!"

Phoebe made the car spin around. "Take the middle of the road and drive at them!" Beatrix commanded. "Hard and fast."

"Not with my car, you don't! You'll get us all killed!" Horace shouted from the back seat.

The two cars were charging toward each other, ever closer to a head-on collision when suddenly the driver of the Comstock car pulled hard to the right, hoping to go around Horace's car, Instead, the car slid on the loose gravel, and the front wheels went off the road. The Comstock car was partially into the ditch.

"Well done, Phoebe!" Beatrix congratulated. "Well done! Now back up carefully to the Comstock car. We'd better see if anyone is hurt. Then turn off the motor and stay put."

Horace got out of the backseat of his car slowly, his pistol in his right hand. Beatrix also had her pistol at the ready.

The driver and two passengers opened their doors. It was little surprise that Mr. Comstock was behind the steering wheel. The surprise was in the back seat.

"Well, Maisie and Daisy, what a surprise to see you again. You've changed your hair color, haven't you? I don't believe you have met my long-time friend and fellow detective, Doctor Beatrix Howell, or my granddaughter, Phoebe. Phoebs was driving. Not bad, was she?" Horace said with a thin tone of triumph in his voice. "All right. Hands up, the three of you. We'll walk you back to your house and we can have a nice little visit. Stay in the middle of the road. Doctor Howell, would you accept the honor of taking the right frank while I take the left. Phoebe, if they try anything, anything at all, just run them down. Hard and fast!" Horace rubbed his finger against his nose to let her know he was not serious.

"By the way, you have seen how she drives. She's fearless, so trust me, she will run you down if you try anything funny," Horace added. "Forward, march. Left, right, left right. That's it. Hands nice and high where we can see them."

EIGHTEEN

"Doctor Howell, this is not the evening I had planned, but still, it's a beautiful evening for a walk," Horace said cheerfully. Before she could answer there was a birdcall coming from the left side of the road. It called a second time.

"All clear, Fred. Come and join us. We're just having an evening stroll back to the Comstock compound."

Beatrix turned to Horace, "You do know how to show a girl an exciting time." They paused on the road, remaining focused on their three prisoners.

There was some rattling of branches in the woods, and suddenly Fred came up the ditch and joined them. "Good to see you, General. You done did have me a little confused with all that fancy driving, and I got a little worried when I heard the car go off the road. Guess it weren't yours, was it?"

"No, not our car. And you'll be happy to know the fancy driving was done by Phoebe. She said it is something called a *Bootleggers Turn* but I guess you being a tee-totaling Methodist wouldn't know about anything having to do with rum runners. Now, what information do you have?" Horace asked.

"I got up close to that there carriage house, but there was a big padlock on the door, like I told you. I knocked on the side walls a few times, and it sounds like there might be someone in there. I figured we were just out on a scouting mission tonight and after I'd reported in we could decide what to do. Looks like you got the jump on me and captured a few of the Hun."

"Yes, meet Mr. Lorenzo Comstock. I think you already know his two daughters, the notorious gold dust twins," Horace said. "Say hello, ladies." They were sufficiently miserable to barely whisper.

"Hello, ladies," Fred said, touching the brim of his fedora. "Say, Doc, what are we going to do with those three?"

"I don't know. I told Phoebs that if they get out of line or try anything funny to run them over. Thunderation, tell me whether or not you found out anything else."

"No sir. Not a thing outside of what I done did tell you."

"Then, I think we make a little diversion across the road to that carriage house and see what's what?" Horace proposed. "You three, halt! Left face. Column left, march. Keep your hands up. Doctor Howell, don't hesitate to use your pistol if they give you any trouble."

When they arrived at the building Horace asked if any of them had the key to the padlock. The trio remained silent. Beatrix cocked her pistol and asked, "Are you sure you don't have the key?"

"It's in the house. In the kitchen on a hook on the wall!" one of the women wailed.

"Horace, this is taking a bit long. Would you please just pick the lock?" Beatrix asked. "Fred, get out your stop watch. I think Doctor Balfour can do the job in under thirty seconds. Phoebe, move the car around so the lights are on the front door of the shed."

Horace was smiling as he unrolled an oilcloth package he had been carrying in his suit. "New set of tools, boss?" Fred asked.

"Yes, a gift from someone who didn't want me ruining dental tools. These are genuine lock picking tools. Let's see, tension rod in first and give it a twist. Next the pick to clear the lock and points. And now the rake. Run it over the pins and twist. There you have it!" When he heard the snap Horace removed the padlock from the hasps on the door. "How long did it take me?"

The two men pulled open the double doors. "Twenty-three seconds, Boss. Let's see what we have here," Fred said.

From somewhere in the building a voice shouted, "Careful. It's booby-trapped! Don't take another step!"

"That you, Nine Fingers?" Horace shouted.

"One and the same, only I want to keep the rest of my fingers!"

"Where are you?" Fred shouted.

"Down here! Shine the light closer to the floor. You see that grate on the floor? The big one, the type that goes under a car?"

"We see it," Horace said.

"Well, you see that can on there?"

"Yes."

"Well, don't touch it. Don't come any closer. Go over to the fuse box and watch out for a trip wire or something, then pull down the handle to make sure the power is off. Get her all the way down, then try turning on and off the light. The switch is right next to the box."

"What does that do?" Fred asked.

"That tin is full of acetate. If the power gets to it and it shorts out on the metal rods I'll be burned alive. Be careful, would you please You see where the wires are on that grate?"

Horace nodded for Fred to pull the switch on the fuse box. "Now, just for safe measure, unscrew those fuses, would you?" Horace asked. "And while you're at it, pull those wires loose."

Horace stepped forward to remove the tin can of acetate when Beatrix stopped him. "No, Horace. Switch places with me and keep the gun on them. I've seen your hands sometimes shake lately which is the real reason you have retired. We will discuss that later. I'm doing this job, so Horace, do as I say, please." Her voice was hushed and urgent.

He reluctantly took her pistol to guard the Comstocks while Beatrix removed the tin of explosive liquid, carried it outside, and poured it on the road to evaporate.

"All you have to do is lift that grate off and I can get out of here. It isn't that heavy," Nine Fingers said. Horace returned Beatrix's pistol to her to help Fred.

As soon as the grate was removed, Nine Fingers moved the ladder into position and climbed out. "Ingenious little death-trap, isn't it? Thank you. I would shake your hand, but I need to clean up and make myself presentable."

"I assume, Doctor Balfour, you no longer believe I am a murderer. That honor goes to Mr. Comstock and his two lovely daughters. Their real names are Bertha and Myrtle."

"Well then, why don't we all go into the kitchen, sit around the table, and get to know each other and catch up on a little history," Horace said. "Phoebe, please pull the car up to the house, and make sure it is facing out. Thank you. By the way, very skilful driving."

She gave him an icy smile, still frightened and feeling very fluttery inside after what she had done.

"The usual adage is for everyone to put their cards on the table. However, I think it would be best if the Comstocks put their hands on the table and keep them there," Beatrix said. They obeyed. "Now, the simple question and answer saves us time. Who shot Mrs. Comstock?"

"I did," Mr. Comstock answered. "I shot her. For years that miserable harpy has yelled and ranted at me, always telling me what I did wrong, that I never did anything right, and that I didn't provide her with enough money. And there is more...." his voice trailed off.

"More?" Beatrix asked.

"Yes. She was the personification of the evil stepmother to my two girls. She was a hateful, spiteful woman. I put us all out of her misery."

"And what about Nine Fingers? What was his role in this?" Horace asked.

"He was the fall guy. The patsy. I could have killed him at the gallery too, but I've known him for a while. Or, I could have said he came here to rob us or something like that and shot him. But I couldn't bring myself do it. That's why he ended up in the carriage house," Comstock said. "I hadn't figured out what to do with him."

"And now that we have that cleared up, I was ah, ah, I was wondering...." Nine Finger's voice trailed off and he gasped for air, his right hand clutching his chest.

"Phoebe! My bag is in the trunk of the car. Now!" Horace ordered. As the girl raced out, Beatrix and Horace helped him sit down, and Beatrix got him a glass of water. Fred kept a close eye on the three Comstocks.

When Phoebe returned, Horace put the stethoscope to Nine Fingers' chest and listened. "Sounds all right. Beatrix, what do you think?"

"I think his heart sounds all right outside of being a bit fast. It could be the shock of his experiences."

"If I am going to live, as it so appears, may I be excused? I would still like to freshen up? It's been a while...." He watched as Horace folded up the stethoscope and put it back into his bag.

"Horace, you keep sharp tools in there, don't you? Maybe I should remove the temptation and put your bag on the kitchen counter. We may need to use them later if our guests aren't willing to talk."

"Yes, by all means," Horace answered. "And Phoebe, I think you should call Bobby at the telephone and have her send Chief Garrison and some extra officers here. Please tell him that we have caught the murderer and his accomplices."

She returned in less than a couple of minutes to report that the chief was on his way.

The Comstocks were quickly arrested and charged with murder. "And where is the notorious Nine Fingers Charlie?" the chief asked.

"He went down the hall to, shall we say, freshen up," Beatrix answered.

Chief Garrison motioned for one of his men to get him. The officer returned, "There aint no one there! Chief, you'd better come see this!" Horace, Beatrix, and Fred were on their feet.

"I don't believe this!" Horace said as he stood in Mr Comstock's office, looking at the open door of the safe.

On the floor next to it was a note. "Thank you for the use of your stethoscope. Nine Fingers."

"Your car!" Beatrix cried out, looking at Horace.

"Phoebe, please tell me you didn't leave the key in the ignition!"

"No! Fred and Beatrix said that was an invitation to a thief." She held up the key on its Masonic lodge fob.

The possibility of a stolen automobile was nothing compared to the look of horror on Mr. Comstock's when the chief brought him into the room to see the safe. "Everything! It's all gone! I'm ruined!"

At first Chief Garrison looked perplexed, then he froze, and started laughing. Not a mere chortle, but a deep laugh, hard and long, that ended only when he began gasping for breath. His face was red, tears dripped off his cheekbones.

"And here you were thinking it was Nine Fingers Charlie who bumped off Mrs. Comstock," he panted, pointing at Beatrix, Fred, and Horace. "I figured it out a long time ago. Nine Fingers Charlie didn't have a thing to do with it. I knew it was Comstock who done it."

Beatrix was about to object, but Horace put his hand on her arm to stop her. "This should be good, seeing how he explains this one," he whispered to her.

"Why sure, see, I had it figured out. Comstock shot his wife in that gallery and hope to pin it on Charlie. That's why it doesn't bother me the least little bit that he's skipped the country. Just like always, I got my man!"

NINETEEN

"Chief, it's getting late, and Phoebe's mother thinks we just went for a drive along the lake. If you don't mind, I'd like someone to drive her home," Horace said.

"Yeah, well it won't be one of you three. I'll have one of my boys do it. And the girl had better stay around town because I've got to get her particulars in the morning," the chief said. He motioned toward one of his officers and told him to drive her home, instructing him to keep an eye out for Nine Fingers Charlie.

Chief Garrison ordered another young policeman to take the three handcuffed Comstocks to the jail in a second car, and then turned to Horace. "You're going to take the lead, nice and slow. My man will be in the middle, and I'll bring up the rear. You're going to drive to the jail and stop and wait there until I get those three in the lockup. After that, you're going to drive straight back to your boat and wait for me while I do the paper work. That clear? I don't want no slip-ups. You park your car right in front of the station and you wait for me to come out. Then you drive to your boat and get aboard and stay there. That clear?"

"What I do not understand is the heavy-handedness of Chief Garrison," Beatrix said once she, Horace, and Fred were in the car. "He has arrested Mr. Comstock for murdering his wife and his daughters as accessories. It does not make sense."

"Whoever said that there chief ever made much sense?" Fred muttered as he drove back to Saugatuck.

"Oh, it makes perfectly good sense. He knows we solved the crime, but he's trying to make sure everyone knows he did it. So, he's controlling the news and will want to make sure our story matches his," Horace said disgustedly.

"Oh, now I understand! He wants to trump us to take the trick!" Beatrix said.

"I don't follow you," Horace answered.

"It's terminology from both whist and bridge," Beatrix answered. "Trump us and take the trick."

She was silent for a few minutes, then said, "Well, that precludes Miss Stymington and Mrs. Vandenberg as suspects, does it not?"

"Disappointed?" Horace asked.

"No, perhaps not. Not entirely. They are unpleasant people, but at least they are not murderesses."

"Not yet, anyway," Horace told her.

"No, not yet," Beatrix agreed. "I won't put it past either of them sometime in the future."

"Now, the first thing I want to know is which one of you three was behind the wheel? I heard there was some pretty fancy driving going on," the chief said as he sat down in a deck chair on the *Aurora* and pulled out his notebook.

"Oh, that was my granddaughter, Phoebe," Horace said proudly. "Quite the Barney Oldfield, isn't she?"

"Phoebe? Don't try to be funny. Now, who was driving?" the chief asked.

All three of them answered in unison, "Phoebe."

"If you must know, Chief, I taught her how to turn the car around while driving," Beatrix said.

"You did? Nah. I taught her how to do it," Fred retorted. "Why, just the other night..."

Horace interrupted, "Knowing you two, you probably both did. Anyway, Chief, the simple fact is that Phoebe was driving. Beatrix was in the front seat with her. Fred and I were in the back, with him on the left side."

"And you were just out for a nice little sunset drive when you captured the murder? Is that your story?" the chief asked.

"Not quite," Beatrix said. "When you have removed the impossible, whatever remains, no matter how improbable, must be the truth."

The chief looked up. "I ought to write that down. It might come in handy some day."

"I would not advise it, Chief. I was quoting Sherlock Holmes from *The Hound of the Baskervilles*," Beatrix said.

"Beatrix, I hate to correct you, but the great detective said it in *The Sign of the Four*," Horace said gently.

She gasped, her face blushing, and she nodded her head in agreement, then smiled. "Ah, but Horace, he said it again in *The Blanched Soldier*, as well."

"Can we stick to the point?" the chief asked in disgust. "It's getting late, you know."

"Of course," Horace said, looking at Beatrix and giving her a slight wink. "We drove down along the lake, and Fred got out to look at the Comstock's carriage house because there was evidence that things were not all as they seemed. We drove along, and they came up hard and fast behind us. As you know, the culvert is out, so Phoebe turned around. Rather quickly, if you want my opinion. They turned around and came after us again, so Phoebe turned around, and they went past us and slid into the ditch. That is when we knew who killed Mrs. Comstock."

"From what he, Mr. Comstock, that is, told us, she had been a vile woman for many years," Beatrix added. "That, however, is hardly justification for taking her life."

For the next two hours the chief peppered Horace, Beatrix, and Fred with questions until he was satisfied with their answers. He yawned loudly and pushed himself out of the chair and on to his feet. "I still got more work to do. I'll be talking to you tomorrow, so stick around town. And your granddaughter better be here when I come calling. Meanwhile, I don't want you talking to nobody about nothing."

The chief's yawn was contagious, and Fred followed his lead. "Bedtime," he announced. "All that excitement sort of leaves a fellow a little tired." He smiled. "But say, we done did some good work, didn't we? Beatrix, I mean, Doctor Howell, good thing we *both* taught Phoebe how to drive."

"Say, I had a hand in that, too, you know," Horace objected.

Beatrix reached over and put her hand on his. "Yes, and when she gets to be a little old lady, then I am sure she will be grateful you taught her how to drive so sedately."

"Good night, Fred. And thank you – good solid work – again." Care for a glass of celebration?" Horace asked Beatrix once they were alone on the deck

"Yes. You did notice, did you not, that once again Chief Garrison was unable to express his gratitude."

"I did," Horace said. "Thunderation! Ungrateful cur, isn't he?"

"Well, I didn't expect to see you again so soon. You might as well know we don't have a safe on the boat," Horace said calmly as he opened the door to his study and found Nine Fingers sitting in a chair.

"How did you get here?" Beatrix gasped. "And why are you here?"

"It's like this. I was out in the country and needed a ride into town, but I was too tired to walk. Lo and behold, there was a car sitting on the side of the road, and the keys right in the ignition. It took a bit of back and forth to get it on the road again, and the next thing I know, here I am in town. I thought I should stop by to return your stethoscope."

"You do know that the police chief would love to arrest you for theft, do you not?" Beatrix asked. "If nothing else, for stealing an automobile."

"Oh, I'm quite certain he would. I parked the car across from the station. I wonder how long he will take to find it. Pity I won't be around. That's why I'm not staying long. I thought your study might be a good place to wait since I'm taking the train out this evening."

"Charlie, there is no train tonight," Horace told him.

"Yes, I know, but the freight train has to slow down when it crosses the bridge just south of here, down at New Richmond. I'm sure they won't approve of it, but they'll give me a lift if I'm careful enough hopping on a flatcar. Of course, a box car might be more comfortable. I found them quite helpful in the past. Anyway, here is your stethoscope back. Now, if you have a spare one, and maybe a black bag you're not using, it might come in handy."

"Wish we could accommodate you, but the answer is 'no,'" Horace said. "Care for a small one?" he held up a glass. Nine Fingers nodded he would.

Beatrix lifted her glass, "Here is to your good fortune of avoiding a murder charge, although I do not approve of your methods of breaking into another person's safe. Why do you do it?"

Charlie looked down for a moment and said, "Well, it's like this. My father worked for Mosler Safe company in Cincinnati, and sometimes he'd let me come in to the factory and see the locks. I found them fascinating, and wanted to work there. The thing was, they wouldn't hire family members because they thought we might be up to no good. You know, passing along information and trade secrets. So, I got a job at a company that published books. Typesetter, that sort of thing.

"Well, I didn't just set the type. I read the books while I was at it. Horatio Alger, Kipling, even old Andrew Carnegie. They whet my appetite for adventure and the good life, and of course, those things cost money; lots of it. I read over a thousand books, everything from art to zoology..."

"Including John Ruskin, correct?" Horace asked.

Nine Fingers rewarded him with a big smile. "Including John Ruskin. And don't let it shock you, but Bob La Follett and a few other Bull Moosers and Progressives. That's when I had a brainwave. All these lawyers who got rich working for the railroads fleecing the working men were trying to hide their money once the income tax came in. And the rum thing is, they kept their money at home because they were scared of bank robbers and safe-crackers, in addition to not letting the feds get wise to them. Isn't that a kicker?" Nine Fingers laughed and slapped his knee.

"Now, Pa had told me most of them had a big safe at home, and I knew how to work the locks, so I decided to, well, redistribute the wealth they were hiding from Uncle Sam. Sort of what the Progressives had in mind, only I was doing the lifting and carrying for them while they did the talking.

"For the benefit of others, I should hope," Beatrix said.

"Well, yes, but I had some expenses of my own. They sort of mount up in a hurry, plus I figured I should pay myself a salary – a generous one, as you can imagine, so there you have it. There wasn't much to splash around like Robin Hood did. He licked his lips as he smiled. "Anyway, it was easy. I worked as a printer so I could make my own calling cards. I had some quality luggage with my initials on it, so I always used a C for the first name and an L for the last."

"Just how did you break into their houses?" Horace asked.

"Break in? Nah, never. That's for amateurs. I was invited in. I am truly proud of that little twist. See, I'd go to museums and art galleries, concerts, places like that, get to meet people, and give them my card. Now, there's no one who wants to boast more about how smart he is than a rich man cheating the government. I'd meet them, wrangle an invitation to call on them or attend one of their society parties, and, well, you can figure out the rest. That's how I got to know Mr. Comstock."

"You robbed his safe?" Horace asked. "I mean, robbed it before tonight?"

"No, he figured it out; me working my way into these swank parties and so on and he offered me a deal. He would turn me in or, we could go into business together. He'd pick the place to hit and let me know when the house would be empty....," Charlie explained.

"For a cut of the action?" Beatrix asked.

"That's about the size of it. See, a fast way to lose money is to open an art gallery, and his Mrs. Had several of them. He said they were all crooked and hiding money from the government. So, they deserved what they got, and they wouldn't squeal to the police because they'd get in trouble with the Feds for evading taxes, you see," Nine Fingers Charlie explained.

"But Mr. Comstock tried framing you for the murder," Horace said quietly.

"Yes, and that surprises me. I guess he figured getting rid of his wife was more important than keeping me as a friend," he sighed. "Turned out he's nothing but a regular cheat. See, when I went down the hall I did a little detour and opened his safe. Well, imagine my surprise when it was packed solid with money, and him telling me how he needed his share. I can't a respect a man who fibs like that, so I thought I ought to teach him a lesson."

"I understand your method, but breaking into a safe is time-consuming, is it not?" Beatrix asked, changing the subject as she held out her glass for Horace to refill. She accepted a cigar with a smile, then lit it.

"Not really, if you know what you're doing. Most safes have three or four tumblers. I use a stethoscope to listen. It's got to be done carefully because what most folks don't know is that these companies add a smaller pin to make a little ping and throw people in my line of business off. Well, I'd read some of Stephen Leacock's books on economics, so I figured out a graph to chart where the numbers are. Turn to the right, find the number; clear; turn left, then turn right again. Chart it and then do it. Just a few minutes, and I'm done and gone."

"All right. I understand the method, but I cannot understand why you were never questioned by the police," Beatrix asked.

"Because no rich man who thinks he has just outsmarted the government by cooking the books to skim money wants the police to know. And they sure don't want their friends to know they were sucker punched in the wallet."

Nine Fingers looked at his pocket watch. "Say, I need to be on my way. It's been a pleasure to get to know you folks, I'm sure." He held up the watch. "Found it laying around in the safe."

"What are your next plans?" Horace asked.

"Oh, I always wanted to try being a broker of rare first edition books. You know, it's only folks with a lot of money who can afford them, and I do know something about books." He laughed, stood up, and left. "Folks with rare books generally got a safe, you know."

"Don't you think we should stop him?" Horace asked once the study door was closed.

"Very likely, we should. He is, after all a criminal. Then again, he did not murder anyone, nor has he ever employed any form of violence in his adventures, and he has an absolutely engaging personality." Beatrix paused and stared at the door. She was motionless for so long the ash of her cigar tumbled onto the carpet. She turned toward Horace and smiled. "You know, we have both enjoyed the Sherlock Holmes stories for a long time. Doyle wasn't the only writer in the family. His brother-in-law was also an author, albeit not nearly as well known. I believe we just met his lead character."

"You've lost me, Beatrix," Horace yawned.

"Doyle's brother-in-law, a Mr. Hornung, wrote the *Raffles* series about a gentleman criminal and thief and his side-kick. Horace, I believe we just met A. J Raffles! I find that very exciting."

TWENTY

"Well, I think we have good reason to celebrate," Horace said as he looked around the dining table. He lifted his water glass. "To good friends, a wonderful family, and new adventures. I'm happy you are here, too, Henry. I understand from Mrs. Garwood that you and your father caught the whitefish we're about to enjoy, so it's only fair you get to help eat them."

"It's a good mess, isn't it, Sir?" Henry beamed.

The others raised their glass and joined him in the toast.

"So, let's see, Phoebe and Harriet, before long it's back to school for you two. You too, Henry. Looks like you get a break from students at Ox-Bow, and Phoebs, looks like you're out of the telegraphing business except on Saturdays. Now I have some other surprises for you. Don't worry, it's all good news!

"I invited Doctor Landis to join us for a very good reason, but I'll explain that in a moment. Moving on: A few weeks ago when Doctor Howell and I were in Chicago to see Colonel McCormick, we had some time before catching the train back here. Well, we went to the restaurant at that new hotel, the Allerton, up on the top floor so we could see all of Chicago, because I had something important to ask her; something that I wanted to talk over with her. I'm happy to say that she liked my ideas..."

Harriet, Clarice, and Phoebe gasped in unison, their eyes widened with anxiety.

Undeterred, Horace continued. "As a result, that means there are some other big changes in the future. Changes that will affect, all of us." He paused to let them spike their anxiety.

"Perhaps both affect and effect all of us," Beatrix added quietly, her eyes down.

"To begin, I bought into Dr. Landis' practice as a partner. As of next month, I'm going to be the town's part time doctor...."

Before Horace could continue, Doctor Landis interrupted, "And with Horace on board, it means we can completely remodel and upgrade the operating room. We're buying the house next door and converting part of it into a much needed laboratory of our own."

There was a round of applause from everyone at the table.

Horace coughed and continued, "Now, rumor has it that some of you have been wondering if I was slipping into my second childhood because I was so interested in that new house being built on Hoffman Street. Well, I had a very for good reason for seeing what was going on. That's the second piece of news. That's my new house. I'm moving here.

"I've always believed that the people in a small town deserve as good a doctor as the people in the big city, so when Dr. Landis opened up a possibility for me, it was too good to resist. If those Young Turks back home want to shove me out to pasture, well, that's their look-out. I'm still a good doctor. So are you Theo. So, there you have it. That's why I'm hanging out my shingle in Saugatuck. Besides, I've come to realize that a day away from Saugatuck is a day wasted..."

Henry interrupted, "Say, I like that! A day away from Saugatuck is a day wasted. I gotta remember that."

"Fred, now, I want you to think this over, but it seems you've taken a fancy to carriage houses, so if you want to re-enlist for another tour of duty, my new place has a carriage house with a big apartment."

"Say, that there is a right good idea. I'll take you up on it, seeing as how you're probably going to need me to get you out of another jam before long! You got it," Fred interrupted. "And, say, I could teach you how to do one of those *Bootlegger's Turn* in case you ever have to use it."

"Wonderful. Thank you, Fred," Horace answered.

"Meanwhile, I'm taking Captain Garwood's advice about the *Aurora* getting a bit elderly for any more trips on the big lake. As old as she is, that big lake is just one big piece of water with a grave carved in it. She was a riverboat on the Mississippi for a lot of years before I bought it, and always will be a river boat. But it is time for her to have an easier life. Captain and I were talking, and he and Mrs. G think it would make a nice tour boat for the Kalamazoo River. If the weather is good, even going out on the lake for a little cruise, long as you stay close to shore. As soon as the house is finished, the boat is all yours. We'll get it into Peterson's dry-dock so she can have a good going over. Meanwhile..." Horace reached into his coat pocket and pulled out an envelope. All yours now."

Everyone watched as Captain and Mrs. Garwood accepted the envelope, hugged and then kissed each other with joy.

"Wait a minute, Grandfather. You're rushing ahead and I'm falling behind. Are you saying you're going to be living here full time?" Phoebe asked. There had been so many surprises she was confused. "And you gave the Garwoods your boat?"

"That's about the size of things. You don't mind, do you?"

In a flash Phoebe completely forgot that she thought of herself as a young lady, became a girl again, and jumped up from her chair to run over to Horace to wrap her arms around his neck. "I think you are the kindest man in the world!"

He chuckled and said, "I guess that means yes."

"Well, Horace, I have a surprise for you," Clarice added. "We feel the same way about Saugatuck, and when we realized you were so entranced by that Sears Roebuck House, Theo and I bought a lot further up the hill, a couple of blocks from you. A fellow named Dahlstrom is drawing up the plans. But seeing as how you're going to be here, we'd better have it made snug for a winter blizzard in case we get invited for Christmas dinner."

"You and Uncle Theo are staying, too?" Phoebe yipped with joy.

"I wasn't planning on going back to work, but you're right about Saugatuck. Don't get me wrong, but spending the summer in that little cabin on the boat gets a bit too much like close quarters. So, we decided... We just didn't know how you'd take it and haven't said anything. So, if you need a first assistant, count on me. Theo said. "And say, Clarice is pretty good passing gas....."

"Would you stop saying that! It isn't polite," Clarice chided her husband. "But yes, I'll be your anaesthesiologist if you need me."

"Now, what about you, Beatrix? You have any surprises up your sleeves?"

Beatrix looked at him blankly and said. "No. I don't keep surprises in my sleeves; just my arms. This isn't much of a surprise but I must return to St. Paul tomorrow, if the weather forecast is favourable. I have to return some papers in the morgue. And, I have a very interesting commission."

"The morgue?" Henry asked. "Isn't that where they keep dead people?"

"Yes, it is, Henry. A morgue is also what they call the library at a newspaper office, and I have some documents I borrowed from a friend who works there. With the arrest of Mr. Comstock and Nine Fingers Charlie's involvement, the reporters will want the documents."

"I sure hope you come back," he said quietly and sadly.

"Henry, that is always the question in life, and sometimes we never know the answer," Beatrix said.

The weather was perfect the next morning, and Horace drove Beatrix to the airfield. "I will be flying around the lake," she told him. "This may sound a bit superstitious, but I thought about that young woman who was flying in the Dole competition from Hawaii to California. Her plane is still missing. It is disconcerting." She paused, then lightly added, "Nor did I want to spike your anxiety. I will send a wire from Chicago and then when I get to Wold Chamberlain in the Twin Cities."

"I'm grateful," Horace said.

"I know," she whispered.

Beatrix was in her flying suit, her leather helmet still unbuckled. She was about to climb into her plane, then paused and turned around to Horace. "I noticed the other day the lot behind your new house went off the market. Perhaps you're getting a new neighbor." She reached out hands to take his. "And just take care of yourself, please."

Before he could answer she turned again and climbed into the cockpit. For a few moments she adjusted some of the control switches, then pressed the starter. Her plane coughed to life, and she used the warm-up time to fasten and adjust the strap on her helmet, and then strapped herself in. With a wave back to Horace, she throttled up the engine and began to taxi to the far end of the landing field. Horace heard the engine come up to power, and then watched as it roared down the grass runway and lifted off.

Beatrix circled once to gain altitude and listen to the engine, and then she began her return trip home.

Made in the USA
Monee, IL
22 July 2021

73670256R00105